—MYSTERY GOTTHEIM—

Five books in THE GOD'S CYCLE

God's House:

Return to God's House
Within Without
In Winter

God's Wilderness:

Mystery Gottheim
Balder's Wilderness

Plus

Gott'im's Monster

GOD'S WILDERNESS

Mystery Gottheim

S. Dorman

~ ~

S. Dorman
P.O. Box 172
Greenwood, ME 04255
USA

(From *The God's Cycle*)

Mystery Gottheim: God's Wilderness
Copyright © 1994-2014 Susan Dorman.
ISBN: 978-0-578-07467-2

Cover design and image by R. and S. Dorman.

Dedication

To Gideon, loved subcreator of Forest Folk

"The heroes of old romance, who went about
smiting dragons, lopping giants' heads, and
otherwise pleasantly diverting themselves,
scarcely deserve mention in comparison with
our New England champions, who, trusting not
to carnal sword and lance, in a contest with
principalities and powers... encountered their
enemies with weapons forged by the stern
spiritual armorer of Geneva. The life of Cotton
Mather is as full of romance.... All about him
was enchanted ground – devils glared on him in
his 'closet wrestlings'...."

—Supernaturalism of New England
John Greenleaf Whittier

Mystery Gottheim

"We don't know why."
   "We don't know why it happened in one night."

~~~~~~~~~~~~~~

Burly Lyman Bearce walked down in the moonlight from one of the Bearces' family timberland parcels, checking on damage to the new logging road—washed out in a torrential onslaught. As always on a mountainous downhill the backs and caps of his damaged knees ached, hobbling him. *Old age. God damn buckets of fun.*

It was cold spring in the early 1980s, wet and leafless. Mud season. There was no one around but the spirits of his yankee ancestors to see him come limping down over the washout of rocks and gravel and sand; no one maybe but them to witness the dark-haired old lumberman in his jacket and hunting cap, his canvas pants and caulked boots, great white beard gleaming on his chest like the moon it reflected. The treetops just off the edge of the road were great pines shadowing the uneven surface here and there, but Lyman Bearce managed to take the view off across the valley where the Arossagunticook gleamed, the flank of great Jasper Mountain showing darkly above with its unready stands of spruce, fir, hemlock and white pine. Even with the painful knees, the late hour, the ravaged road surface, Lyman Bearce was strong and ready enough on his legs to pay but scant heed to how he went. Instead he looked off at the great things of God reflected in the moonlight of another blesséd Gott'im evening, now well into night. And so it was that he saw there across the river valley a road he'd never seen before, cut like a thin white scar in the conifer wood on the lower west side of the mountain.

And Lyman Bearce stopped. *What in hell—a road?*

He was a local lumber baron, almost bigger than anybody: He had forty thousand acres if he had a foot of timberland. At the moment he was not even sure exactly just how much he had, that's-how-much-he-had. And Lyman Bearce knew this part, he knew this county. He would have said he knew every road in every mountain between here and Lord's Hill to the southwest, in New Hampshire.

The first thing he thought was *Liquidation Leo*, Leonard Guerette. He was gobbling up land—not just stumpage—from the paper companies the last few years, and was beginning to encroach into Western Maine. Bearce did not stop long in his hobbling descent, but he was busy over who owned that parcel. His mind just wasn't working now. *Old age. Buckets of goddamn fun.*

He came to the next opening and, sure enough, the cut was still visible, gleaming like a thread he could reach out to grasp and follow. Wonder where it would lead? That timber's not ready, he thought.

Champion, Woodland, Great Northern, Scott. He ticked them off on his fingers, not bothering to ask himself why the name Guerette was the first thing in his mind. Adirondack Paper was sure to be next. Yes, he thought that section over there belonged to them. Guerette was the next big enemy—an independent contractor! *Hell.* Lyman Bearce ate logging contractors in this county, and halfway to the middle of the state, for breakfast. But here was Liquidation Leo taking advantage of the state of the industry, the unlooked for passing of the great companies into other, less considerate, hands. Great out-of-staters and internationalists who cared nothing about— about—about how to *do* a thing!

Guerette would turn that side of the mountain into a melt down—timbers flowing like milk from a cow. Jasper Mountain— cash cow! He was clambering down the washout apace now, fists clenched, shoulders fixed, as he searched out his footfalls to get below to the Blazer. What was he going to do when he got there? Hop in and drive along the river ten miles to the bridge, backtrack ten miles, search out some obscure gate from any of the many miscellaneous deadend lanes going up the side of the mountain? It was impossible. What was he going to do, roll in at 3:00 a.m. and have the old girl asking him where in hell he'd been? *Old age. You go crazy too. God damn buckets of fun.*

~~~~~~~~~

"The intellectual are different to I and you," paraphrased Eloise Patadoe out loud where she lay prone overlooking the edge of a cliff. In the same moments when Lyman Bearce began fuming over the apparition of a thin white line on Jasper Mountain, she had cast off her pack and was high above on the same mountainside, chuckling gleefully over the opening line in her proposed illustrated comic novel. "They suffer a low threshold of boredom, catching on quickly and conserving their skins."

....It needed work. Maybe it should be businessmen... or entrepreneurs. Or high school principals... or – It can't be the rich because that's been done. She could see it needed work but not with clarity, being too easily enamored of her creativity. Scarcely regarding the rocks, twigs and spongy lichen, she rolled over onto her back and looked up at the washed out stars. There was too much moonshine to see and feel the grip of their wonder this night, too much wash to make much interest.

Ah, she sighed, it's nice to be back from New York City, back in Gott'im where the emperor is forced to wear clothes or have a sense of humor about himself. She could feel her lanky ponytail hanging over the edge of rock collecting bits of this and that, the rock supporting her neck, the lichen cushioning her head. She recalled briefly how the village had failed to appear immediately she hit the curve of the highway where you first catch a glimpse of it. After being all night on the road, she had found only a thick black mist in the morning. The village had been disposed of—again. Ever since Ceylon Segar's tire fire, the village had drifted in and out of apparent existence. She had heard tales of people just missing it, bypassing an invisible Gottheim all together on their way to ... wherever. A couple of her artist friends had failed to materialize for a visit once on account of this.

She inched backwards a bit, letting her head lay over the edge of the precipice, her ponytail hanging down its face. Mouth agape, her bespeckled eyes rolling back, she looked across at the mountain, the same flank that had so irritated Lyman Bearce who was well below her now, hobbling down the washed out road.

Ah, Jasper Mountain. You're upside down.

She could not see its rounded summit from here but she scrutinized with the alert observant eye of an artist the dark conifer flank across the way, spotting here and there the glint of mica or pegmatite in its outcroppings. Do you know, she said to it, there is a zany movement afoot by the local neo-witches to begin some sort of worship of you? She sighed. An exaggerated sigh. All of Eloise's sighs are exaggerated. *Why can't people just treat you like the normal great being you are?* You've got your Goldings and your paper companies treating you like a gold mine (let alone the actual miners mining you for beryl, topaz and tourmaline); skiers using you like a playground, jumping on you like a trampoline; now the silly believers are thinking you're some kind of god (it's not like they're Native Americans or anything). The only people who use you normally (besides my own gracious self) are the descendants of settlers who live on you. ... But you are upside-down more and more, aren't you? ... You look strangely so, with your head in the stars of earth and your feet in the heaven of the river rapids.

Eloise heard a faint scratching and inched backwards towards the woods. Now she lolled over onto her side, staring into the mysterious shadowed tangle.

"Here, Sheila," she said. A black goat came out of the shade and puckerbrush and began licking her cheek and glasses, knocking them askew with her cross-shaped dark pointed face. One of her small polished horns was perilously close to gouging out her owner's eye as she went on licking.

Eloise and Sheila were up on the ledge ostensibly to scout out the townline, but it was rare that Eloise bypassed an opportunity to see anything from a new perspective. She had spent most of the day hiking through puckerbrush and swamps and over beaver dams, slogging the occasional small bog and hunting through woodland, trying to decipher the true boundary line, shared with Quaker and Gottheim. Not that Eloise had much land, but she had gotten curious about the land beyond. This led to curiosity about the boundary of the two towns. With her were compass and topographical map and lunch and a goat. Sheila could be a pretty good companion if the coy dogs were on the other side of the mountain.

Now Eloise sat up and began rubbing her lenses with the tail of her shirt. Then she stood, stuffed it back into her overalls and jacket, and brushed herself off; now carefully scrutinizing shoes, socks and the cuffs of her overalls. "Let me check you, too," she said to Sheila. "We don't want to go swapping bodily fluids with ticks, do we?"

It was time to wander back home into Quaker from the margin of Gottheim. She thought she had seen a logging road down below somewhere. Eloise and Sheila went back into the woods, never having seen any sign of a cut, the line of silver indicating a road on the opposite flank that had so infuriated Lyman Bearce.

Moonlight in the woods is her undoing—as an artist and as a person. She tries to capture her experience on canvas, on paper, in collage, gouache, charcoal pencil pen and ink. The shadows are blackly evocative, rich, slanting back below the white of trees dressed in moonshine. The quality of black and white is all you get, what you perceive even if shades of gray and silver and selenium toning do reside in these colorations. *It should be so easy, but I fail.*

Eloise sighed. And I can never get enough of this, the haunting overwhelming mystery of moonlight woods: it needs forever, an infinity of experience—no time out. *At the full moon I have to be here.* Have to creep around, get renewed by this mystery.

Everything was damp, and fragrant of duff and earth. Sheila meandered through the blowdown and puckerbrush and beneath twisted dead limbs of cedar, her mistress always a little before her. That strange woman who never took time to munch on lichen or nibble arborvitae. The goat looked like a wandering black misshapen shadow following in the wake of the white lady in white-seeming jacket and overalls.

Eloise clambered over deadfall and then the descent began asserting itself. The wet leaves were slick and treacherous. She took handholds on branches and saplings and the rough trunks of ash, the smooth of beech or knobby birch. In the mystery of moonlight she'd gotten away from the ledge and now the woods deepened and she felt she had lost the opportunity of the road. At least Sheila seemed to be enjoying herself on the downhill, her nimble cloven hooves grasping hold of rocks and roots, while Eloise had to concentrate on how she went through the trying mystery of woodland descent.

It gentled some and then she saw the deer, one of which was small and white. They followed deer, but at a distance until the deer startled and leapt away. All but the white one. It led them on. Later Eloise found it leading to rocks that had a straight-edged human-made look to them. She realized that she was looking at gravestones akilter: narrow rectangular slabs, some still standing crookedly, others flat on their backs or faces among the stems of seedlings and the duff of leaves and pine needles. And on all sides the woodland had grown up around this settlers' and descendants of settlers' graveyard, overcome by the growth of a century, washed but not righted in the mystery of moonlight, the frightening white moonlight. "This is the best ... Sheila," she whispered. The white deer was gone.

She let it all in: the blacks and whites of the moony boneyard with the bare trees overhead weaving their stark limbs in the moonlight that was broken and darkened here and there by shadows of conifers. Many of the slabs were blackened by decades of lichen and mold, but some were still clean and white, upstanding and hardly weathered: the slate ones, she supposed. The ground was somewhat springy beneath her feet, surprising her, for one mostly feels the rock of New England, the hard bones of the country wherever one walks. In the rear hunched a large dark form. Backed by tall thickets of shading fir. At first she thought it was an erratic, the ponderous leaving of glaciers from lands far to the north. But as she neared and her eyes adjusted to the gloom, she saw it was a vault of hewn unmortared granite, its great lintel large and heavy beneath the stone roof deep with duff and sprouted seedlings. Approaching it she was shocked by a sudden jolt to the shin and, glancing down, saw what at first sight looked like a human tibia beneath the old leaves. At that moment Sheila nudged her from behind and Eloise shrieked.

She knelt on one knee and put her arm around the goat's neck, hugging it and burying her face in the soft wool.

"Sheila, I thought it was a leg bone .... I really did."

Rummaging around in an old New England graveyard will do that if you must go creeping through woods in the moonlight.

She sat back on her haunches still leaning against the goat and looked again at the thing. Mesmerized, she picked it up.

I'm holding in my hand the leg bone of a human being. I'm holding in my hand the leg bone of a human. I'm holding in my hand.... Then she thought about the laws of physics and wondered what had made it jump up and hit her. She held its knobby end out into a shaft of moonlight, surmising that she had leveraged it into her shin as she went. *The leg bone's connected to ...* went running through her mind and she started to her feet—feeling the creaking of her knees and creep of fear play through her nerves—wondering what else she might find.

At first she nudged at the duff with her foot, but then she picked up a stick and started stirring through it slowly; like a woman with a metal detector looking for gold. Stirring the dank ground made her sneeze and cough. Her finds were scattered but various: large and small finger bones (some misshapen from arthritis, others tiny and delicate as a baby's); a jaw without teeth, a broken calcified shoulder bone. Granting their strange beauty, she liked the look of them all lined up neatly in a swatch of moonlight upon one face-down gravestone.

It was a trail of bones leading to the door of the vault: which was slightly ajar. She stopped stirring the duff upon realizing this trend.

Sheila was dining on the edges of the graveyard beneath the ghostly white oaks, but it was a narrow burying ground, and Eloise said to her across its crazy dishevelment, "I'm not going in there.

"This is a boneyard, now, is it not? A yard where bones are piled and stacked, but they are supposed to be kept out of sight of our delicate eyes, letting the worms do their worst in private, as becometh the pathetic creatures, woman and man."

Sheila said nothing. She chewed cud from one of her stomachs. Eloise was not sure which stomach, never having learned the exact anatomy of the creatures under her care. "Maybe I should sit here like Shakespeare and muse aloud upon these things, chewing the coughed up cud of the intellect, seeing what's below in my helter-skelter unconscious." But then it came into her mind, *The intellectuals are different than you and I ... catching on quick and preserving their skins.*

Leaving most of the beautiful white pieces, she walked over to the goat to lead her away. Together they walked on through the silent rich configuration of moonlight and woodland shadow, the human murmuring, "... Why couldn't they keep their skins?"

Eloise had a long way to go that night through the black and white of the rising full moon and deep woodland; on and on toward the Quarry Dog Road where she lived with her goats and her paints. She had a lot to occupy her mind which moved from one thought to the next, thoughts changing hands like partners in an old-time dance. There was an old-time dance coming up she hoped to attend; in what had once been the Quaker Plantation townhall. After tonight's experience Eloise realized she would be changing hands in the dance with skins full of finger bones.

Besides the bones in the boneyard Eloise thought of the upcoming straw poll, to be held in the same hall, meant to decide on a move to turn back the township's legal status to that of Plantation. This was preparatory to preventing a backer of Native Americans, at the other end of the state, from building a high-stakes bingo parlor in their midst. She thought then of her other discovery, made during the early evening; one that suggested an error in the boundary between the Town of Gottheim and Quaker township. With increasing weariness in dismay, again and again as she worked her way toward what she hoped was the direction of her little homestead, failing to find and take Lyman Bearce's new logging road back down to Quarry Dog Road. How simple the night would have been. How lacking in bothersome complexity, how restful. After all the multifarious twists and turns of New York City, with its intense and troublesome physical exertion of mounting a show in some almost nameless gallery, she had craved the uncomplicated quiet of Quaker and Gottheim.

No, unlike her friends from away, she would not have missed Gottheim even shrouded in a pall. What a euphonious name, she thought: spelled S-E-G-A-R, but pronounced cigar. Ceylon Cigar. The burning of Ceylon Segar's tire fire continued apace, mingling its soot, oil fumes blackness and stench with rain and mists. It dampened all the excitement of the ski resort and its accompanying development. The little great grubby Ceylon Segar with his pathetic great grubby machinations had inadvertently managed to best the great shining, decidedly ungrubby Goldings by converting the treasure ground of Jasper Mary into a tire dump for millions of America's castoffs.

"Could anything be worse for the legend of Jasper Mary than a monumental tire dump with millions of tires?"

Locals had opined it before freak lightning extended the inquiry to include natural disaster. Could anything be worse for Eloise Patadoe than to discover the bones of a dead person on top of a grueling and complicated week? How about discovering the bones of dead *people*? Would that be enough to agitate and discompose a deceptively phlegmatic personality?

While down below, riding off in his car, another soul wondered. Could anything be worse this night for Lyman Bearce, besides bad knees and a washed out road than an apparent new cut in the side of Jasper Mountain? How about that plus a wife confronting you at 3:00 a.m. with irritating questions?

But all these things are merely troublesome and soon able to be comforted away with hot baths and whiskey with a beer chaser, or a cup of herbal tea with a bite of goat milk cheese followed by a sound night's sleep. It's not quite enough for a savoury story featuring at least one descendant of the old settlers who routed the Indians and drove them, crowding, into remote corners. It's not enough for a woman from away who was essentially meant to live on the edge. There is no real challenge in this. It needs more. It needs the writing finger of a storyteller who knows much about mystery, human nature, and hidden treasure. It needs the writing finger of a Jesus of Nazareth, the stylus of a Virgil, or tongue of a Jasper Mary: It needs a shifting and sifting of the winds.

~~~~~~~~~~

The Village of Gottheim glowed faintly, fitfully, in a dark fold of the old hills. From one of the new houses perched on a ledge overlooking it beneath the faded stars, the village looked sinister. Like some volcano crusted over in colder lava and moving with its furnace hidden beneath. Its line of street lamps on Front Street could be faintly guessed, and most of its houses and all of its stores were dark— if a couple of its nightspots *were* open underground. But there was one light on its edge unobscured by the moving cloud of soot and mist hovering over Gottheim's ponds and treetops and byways.

Descend from the ledge where the new house stands, to the field and railroad tracks at the edge of the village, there to see a light high against the moving dark upon a knoll. Crazy Knoll it was called, filled with old and in some cases rundown Victorian mansions and houses. Here was a lane which twisted this way and that without apparent rhyme or reason, ultimately twisting back upon itself to exit from the same point of its entrance in the village proper. Tonight Crazy Knoll, as on many other nights, was mercifully spared the pall which frequented other parts (troubling the respiratory systems of certain sufferers and clinging obscurely to the exhaling pond waters). High in a tower upon the edge of things was that one light, the light of the village eccentric and hermit. His name was Israel Kimball.

Israel Kimball was the town's biggest busybody and know-it-all, though nobody knew it. Anybody would have laughed at the idea and ridiculed his informant into the ground. "That old recluse? Nobody's heard so much as two peeps out of him in three decades at least. Unless his niece is going around under cover of darkness listening beneath windows and at keyholes, he can't know a thing what's going on in Gott'im—but what he might read in the bellyache if he had a mind to. Which he wouldn't. How do we even know he's still alive? Maybe he's been dead the last decade and no one knows it. Maybe his niece goes up into the tower and turns on the light every night to make everyone think he's still up there. Maybe he's really down in the cellar, or the subcellar might we say? Not that she'd do away with him or anything but he's in his 90s if he's a day— maybe even his 100s! A person could die in that condition."

Though not so old as Israel Kimball, these would be the old timers talking, those of his niece's generation. Most people in Gottheim knew little enough of Israel Kimball. A few of them knew that his shabby old mansion was home to some students at the academy, the poorer variety, those on scholarship. Housing them was how his niece earned a living. That and a few other odds and ends of jobs she had, like taking in laundry, sewing, things like that. Israel Kimball used to teach at the academy himself. In his day he was thought very learned if quiet, imparting his learning only to the scholars.

And up there, in that six-sided tower, high above everything else in the village—that's where the one light glowed. And there Israel Kimball was reading the bellyache and praying after every few paragraphs. And there Israel Kimball was stopping to meditate upon the great tire fire of Ceylon Segar; and there too, he mused upon that one's grubby old soul. And then when he got done doing that, he began to give thanks for the disaster that had brought death and plague, and blighted the entire quality of life in the beautiful white New England village of Gottheim in the beautiful Western Mountains of Maine. After that he gave thanks for the rats.

~~~~~~~~~~~~~~

Before his mind turned to the subject of rodents, Daniel Twitchell had been walking along the Lower Intervale Road in the light of the fabulous full moon. It was one of his favorite things to do, though he was more rarely conscious of the fact. There had been an impromptu party down by the river at the Old Ferry Landing near a deserted farmhouse, the site long disused and abandoned but still relevant as part of the town's history. He had seen swaths of the gleaming river in passing along the road that was interspersed with one small working farm or another and thick dark clumps of woodland. But now he turned off into the rich suggestive shade of the forest on the long dirt track winding up toward the beat-up old truck camper he shared with his family: Mother, stepfather, and brothers Nathan and Benaiah. He thought maybe the rats were busy sneaking back into the household. He did not know if Peter would be with them much longer.

Of course Daniel was not drunk, though there had been drinking and reefer at the party. He did not drink or smoke pot but, if he had been so inclined, it would have been disastrous to show up with even the faintest sniff of alcohol on his breath. They were all probably asleep anyway, he thought; but then his mind took another turn, for the moonlit woods would have its influence upon him. How alive with blacks and whites and dark mysterious shapes, with a webwork of light and shade arcing the gray track on either side as he began to climb. It was spooky.... It was *sinister*....

Daniel was thinking about that word sinister. He had to think about words, he was going to be a writer, maybe a journalist, maybe a poet. He did not know which but he did work after school at the local print shop of *The Village Voter* for Mr. Nutting, the editor. And he had been thinking a lot about words because he had to set up words for the press, so letters were always before him in some form or other. He was a reader as well. But that word *sinister*: it was meant for these woods. And now Daniel thought it was weird that the word had originally stemmed from left-handedness. No other 15-year-olds in his class would know this about *sinister*, he thought. They would not know that he knew this oddity about that word. To them his job at the local weekly was just an after-school job, a way to earn money. To Daniel it was a way to get out of Gott'im some day. I am left-handed, thought Daniel. Does that mean I'm sinister? He almost half-smiled.

Now, as he climbed through the overarching tunnel of woven branches with its patterns of light and dark, he thought again about rodents. Not about the rats that had taken up residence wherever they might in fleeing the tire fire, but about Mr. Mason's survey of the local ground hog population. This interested Daniel enough to want to try and sell Mr. Nutting on the idea of a feature story about it. Of course Daniel had never done anything like it before and this was rightfully Libby's job; he might be considered to be undercutting her if he suggested it in connection with himself. But at least he could suggest it and hope that Mr. Nutting might take the hint, grant him the opportunity.... Especially if he fleshed out a presentation.

...Which would go something like.... "Remember I told you about our biology class working on that groundhog survey? Well, it turns out we may even be turning in our data to the Department of Environmental Sciences at the University of Maine.... Mr. Mason says not to count on its being used before its quality is assessed.... The students are helping a behavioral ecologist determine what makes them solitary—the groundhogs, I mean. She's working on her doctorate, I guess. I mean she is. She *is* working on her doctorate."

He tried rehearsing it, placing emphasis, even memorizing it, but then realized this was no good. Such strategies never worked for him. He would just have to wing it and *hope* it was good enough.

The woods kept distracting him from these plans anyway. He had come up the track many times after dark but it had a stark romantic luster tonight and he realized that every night the walk had been somehow different; that nothing was ever the same. Its shapes, so familiar in the morning when they came down to get the school bus, seemed to morph through night's changing atmosphere, its variety of darkness and light .... Spooky.... Sinister... but not with evil; more with... what?—expectancy? Here is that old logging track he had meant to follow one day just to see if any changes had occurred since last summer. Not that he expected any. From here all looked completely unchanged, covered in leaves and pine needles, starting to grow over.

On impulse he decided to cut away with it. He might end up in the puckies, but at least he would be below camp and able to work his way up past the sapping ground were the evaporator sat under wraps after serving its first great sugaring-off—to the profit, Mother said, of the entire family. Here the trees on either hand had not grown up so thick as on the main track. The night above was bright, its stars barely visible, but the clear disc of the moon was cut off by a shoulder of Blackwell Mountain.

He went deeper and deeper along the bright track. Up ahead was a big old stump, probably a mossy old stub, lopped off long ago, not in the more recent cut that was only a decade or two old. But, as he approached, he saw what looked to be a manmade shape on the stump. The stump was not out in the moonlight, but under the shade of some evergreens; yet he recognized that here was either a block of wood— or a book. Yes, a book it was.

Sinister .... "Presaging trouble; ominous." He almost half smiled.

Daniel Twitchell approached and picked up the old book with a tentative gentle hand. He could see right off that was not in the best condition. Even though it was somewhat watermarked it was now dry, which surprised him. The weather had been rainy or misty. Without taking his eyes off its cover he walked out into the light of the night and opened the book, softly flipping its pages to test its condition. The leaves held to the spine and he closed it and read its title and author: Phantastes by George MacDonald.

Phantastes, he thought. Related to fantasy.

Suddenly there was more light and he looked up to see the moon apparently slipping from behind the shoulder of Blackwell and now shining through the webwork of the trees. There was enough light to read its text if he cared to, even as he walked along the track. He had often whiled away the long climb up Blackwell Mountain toward Buck Hill with a book, beating back his small boredom with it, but he was not of a mind to do any such thing now. He did, however, stand there a moment to sample it. He was certainly going to keep the book. You don't just find something like this on a stump every day and walk past leaving it for the mice to eat. He knew from time spent at his grandmother's house that mice would nibble the thing to bits and probably enjoy its glue for a treat.

The book was open at random, and Daniel read:

All this time, as I went through the wood, I was haunted with the feeling that other shapes, more like my own size and mien, were moving about at a little distance on all sides of me. But as yet I could discern none of them, although the moon was high enough to send a great many of her rays down between the trees, notwithstanding she was only a half-moon. I constantly imagined, however, that forms were visible in all directions except that to which my gaze was turned; and that they only became invisible, or resolved themselves into other woodland shapes, the moment my looks were directed towards them. However this may have been, except for this feeling of presence, the woods seemed utterly bare of anything like human companionship; for I soon found that I was quite deceived; as, the moment I fixed my regard on it, some form showed plainly that it was a bush, or a tree, or a rock.

Daniel looked up from the page in his hand at the bright track now barred and detailed with shadows laid down by the trees before the moon. He looked off on either side, noticing the shapes of bushes or trees or rocks or blowdown. He grimaced and closed the book with a snap of finality in his two hands.

Suddenly he was aware of the sounds. He had not been noticing noises since leaving the cheeping of peepers behind sometime before on the road below: His own thoughts had been too loud. But now the atmosphere of the moony woodland overtook him. Whispers threading through the pines above him on his left hand sounded almost too suggestive to bear. He looked at his hand holding the book and switched hands, shoving the offending left hand into his pocket.

He held the book to the light again, reading its faded curlicue lettering. *Phantastes: A Faerie Romance for Men and Women.*

What in heck is this book doing out here?

It had not occurred to him to wonder this even when he first saw it on the stump.

He started on again, this time aware of passing woodland shapes and the sounds of night: from the owl way off in the woods below, gently questioning, to the persistent lonely muted chirping in the shadows on his right: nebulous rustlings, rhythmic creakings, faint crackings and droppings, as though the woods had nothing better to do than let things down from above. Random noises in the woods intensified until he felt himself one big ear to receive it all. He was also an all-eye to receive the dark suggestive richness of the woodlands' Being, the great bright Being of the Moon through teeming black branches—nothing had ever been so evident as this mountainside in the night. Its mounting nonhuman intensity seemed about to reft his identity.

A disembodied enchantment began setting him apart from it all, even as he looked down and saw his strange sneakered feet moving rapidly over the duff and twigs and debris of the track. Were they his feet?

~~~~~~~~~~~~

Earlier in the same evening, Asa Bartlett and his wife, Olive Lovejoy Bartlett (who once had the keeping of a few mentally disabled), were on their way back from the old meetinghouse where the Gottheim Historical Society usually met. There was a nice full moon —and so they had ridden to the white meetinghouse, with the his-and-her doors, on a pair of Asa's great old bays. They were now *clip-clopping* single file back home on the shoulder of the road along the river between the old hills. Everything was silvered over with moonlight: the intermittent fields and woodlands, the occasional house or farmstead with extended dwelling—house-ell-barn. Sometimes the river was visible in the distance, pouring back moony reflection into their eyes or a dark surface untouched with direct light. Once they moseyed through a deep tunnel of trees where a lane intersected leading through deep dark down to the river, and then they heard the remote sound of frenetic music driving itself up to their ears from some boombox down at the hidden Old Ferry Landing.

"Kids is havin'a party down theya," observed Olive over her shoulder to Asa.

He saw her plump profile beneath her battered fedora. She looked more stylish than usual in a belted trench coat. He said, "Wish they'd choose some otha place. Those kids'll end up burning down history one o'these days."

"If wishes were horses ...."

He knew she would answer him thus. They hadn't been married a year, but of their nearly sixty as friends, he knew pretty much what she was bound to say.

Things didn't change that much, he knew. There was a pattern to personality, to relation, to history, to the generations and how they were bound together; a pattern, just like there were patterns of seasons or weather or a fine piece of workmanship or a song. Human nature, he believed, was stuck in one God awful pattern, for sure. No force but God's own could change that. Kids were bound to either burn down or overturn history, make that pendulum swing, because that's what kids were bound to do. He still didn't know but what they hadn't set that tire fire, though that crackpot artist from away swore up one face of Jasper Mountain and down its backside that they didn't do it. He had no evidence her word wasn't trustworthy, but then he didn't know her well enough to know otherwise, either. She was just too talky smiley, what they call flaky, and know-it-all to be trusted. Asa was not going to share these ruminations with Olive. That too was predictable—as he already knew she liked Eloise Patadoe, which counted the same as approval with Olive.

He looked at his wife's large back on the large bay, both almost as plain as day in the moonlight. Together they went moseying up the spine of the road and into the trees again. But as they were coming out to the open at the top of the hill, by the intersection with Quakertown Road which ran back into the hills, they heard what sounded like the rumble of iron-bound wheels… from a great distance. They heard the remote thundering of hooves on hard-pan, and a far off panting of horses. And they looked down there and they saw.

It was one sight they neither of them had seen before, and when it got done with them they neither of them hoped they would see it again, though they always would ever after.

Later Asa thought that the seeing and the hearing were not put together right. It was as though what they *heard* was coming to them over a great distance or through tunnels under the earth or maybe from some distant star. But what they *saw* was coming like an avalanche tumbling rocks and trees and the great side of a mountain down on them. It was a pair of great Belgians with what looked to be a stagecoach or freight carrier tearing down a rise toward them as they stood stupefied at the intersection of the Lower Intervale and the Quakertown roads.

Their bays were old and they were old horsemen themselves; instinctively they gripped their great mounts and held them steady. For, in their spookery, even the horses acknowledged the apparition. Apparition it had to be though it looked to Asa as solid and convincing as Olive herself coming toward them. If driver it was—all bundled together in the shape of a man topped with a bowler—at the last moment, he geed his Belgians away toward

Gottheim, and they heard him imploring, but again as though from that distant star, *Gee! gee! lay 'em away! Lay 'em away my townsmen!* The lips muffled beneath the bowler may have been moving, but the adjuration came not from the driver before the box. And then it was gone, that great long box of a carriage with its lathered and furious steeds. Stupefied still, Olive and Asa watched its backside receding, now but a dark rectangle between the thin lines of its wheels, two lights barely showing high upon either side in the light of the moon.

Suddenly they were alone and awake on the Lower Intervale Road.

"...You saw that, I s'pose," said Olive, whose bay was ponderously dancing beside his.

"What? Oh that. Yuht, I saw it."

"Ever seen it before?"

"I don't think so."

They moved on up the road together, side-by-side, slowly, toward Gottheim in the wake of they knew not ... —*what* to call it?

"Ever seen such a long carriage in any of your books on such things?" She wondered aloud. "Or in person?"

"How would *you* describe it?"

"Kinda like a traveling medicine show ... or ... something. Except granda."

"Could'o been fah a medicine show—except fah the driver's elevated seat ... and that glass paneling ... and the gilding and was it red?— drapery."

"Guess you saw it good enough....Way too fine."

Asa and Olive went on clopping along the road toward Gottheim.

"Whad you s'pose he was saying?" wondered Olive.

"Was that him saying it?"

"Well, I don't know but I s'pose maybe."

"—It couldn't 'o been a.... 'twas all too solid fah a ghost, that. ...Wouldn't you say?"

Olive didn't answer right off. Then she said, "What else could it'o been? Not makin' a sound like that?... Not that I know much about... ghosts. Firsthand. D'you?"

They were both feeling their way along the road back to Gottheim. Feeling their way with their words, not really looking at the hot-top or the moon or the trees or fields or each other, just feeling their way with their words.

"Would I say if I did?"

Now she did look at him sidelong. "I b'lieve you would, Asa. If I 'memba right you gave a pretty good talk on the subject, complete with stories, last summer."

"Not my stories. And they mostly came out of the old books and papers. Hardly anyone around here owns such sights anamore .... But this wasn't anathin I've heard anywhere. —You know there was something familiar about it...."

Olive sighed and they moseyed on. After a bit, she said, "Should we tell anaone?"

Asa could have predicted the question. He might have asked it himself. Some things are predictable, he guessed; most things aren't. He would not have predicted that he would soil himself riding Elmer on his way home tonight, for instance.

No need to tell Olive, he thought. She might find out soon enough.

But not if he can help it.

~~~~~~~~~~~~

Daniel has come back into his body, recovered his senses, recognizes his own feet again. He finds himself breathing heavily, slowing down, still on the track bright and wide in the moonlight, full of small growing things. It's going to take a jog up ahead, he reminds himself, and he'll have to go on straight into the puckies. It should be no problem ... just keep alert, pay attention to the lay of the land. It's all uphill after that. No sweat.

He looked again at the book in his hand, at the shadows of the woodland, the great shining moon. Now the moon reassured him and he felt foolish over his momentary imaginative lapse. He reminded himself that he likes walking alone at night in the moonlight far from the city. Sometimes when the woods encroached, he missed the desert outside Phoenix: There was the place to be warmed by the moon! He liked the desert better than the Maine woods, but it was Mother's choice and there was nothing he could do about it. Besides, it was not a choice between the city and the desert: Mother and Petey never would have been able to afford a place in the desert. Now they were here and that was that....

Or was it?

Sometimes he wondered if Peter Prince was going to be able to stand living here. Sometimes he thought maybe his stepfather would blow again as he used to in the old days. If he did he would start drinking, start treating Mother bad all over again, and then what would they do? Was there any place to run after Gottheim? The good Peter, led by the bad Petey, would probably find them again wherever they went. Or was it the other way around: the good Peter leading? Daniel had not figured it out yet. He didn't like to just consign Peter to Hell. He had been good to them most of their lives. Have to recognize that. He can make life hell, and he can make it normal. It amazed him that people had such power over the quality of everyone's life.

He looked again at the book, Phantastes. What a way to spell it. It made him think of the oddity that was language and how it could make you see things differently, make you feel things you didn't know you felt.

He opened the book again at random and read,

> *Meantime, how fared Cosmo? As might be*
> *expected in one of his temperament, his interests*
> *had blossomed into love, and his love—shall I call it*
> *ripened, or—withered into passion? But, alas! he*
> *loved a shadow.*

... Must be a metaphor. Nobody would love a shadow.
He read on, trying to get a glimpse of what the writer was talking about.

> *Nay, how many who love never come nearer than*
> *to behold each other as in a mirror; seem to know*
> *and yet never know the inward life; never enter the*
> *other soul; and part at last with but the vaguest*
> *notion of the universe on the borders of which they*
> *have been hovering for years?*

Maybe marriage is meant to do something about this (yeah common-law marriage). But watching Mother and Peter together Daniel had yet to see much sign of it.... Either they did not know each other, or were no good at communicating what they did know. ...Although he thought maybe Mother was closer to understanding Peter. In a way it was kind of like the way Mr. Mills understood the weather—because he was a farmer and had to know how to get around it. Daniel did not think he knew what made Peter tick, but he did know when weather was coming. —Ticking was too much like clockwork to describe Petey, anyway.

Daniel slid back into the book again at random and began reading about the Ash-tree and its shadow. The first-person narrator seemed to be somehow menaced by it.

There were plenty kinds of trees in the woods, he knew: he was sure Mother had mentioned ash trees before, something about using them to make baskets. She was going to try getting into her Native American heritage. Daniel was indifferent to it; he was indifferent to kinds of trees. Trees are trees, rocks are rocks and puckerbrush is puckerbrush, that's all .... But now he wonders about ash trees.

He scanned the hardwoods to see if he recognized anything there. The woods were taller, scarcely any budding branches up there. He noticed different kinds of bark in the moonlight. Some of it smooth, some ragged, some knotted, some ridged. All kinds of trees, and of course he recognized the birches but could not tell the gray from the paper birch. *I'm not going to know which of these trees is an ash tree. If there is one.*

He realised now that he didn't know much of anything about the woods yet. Maybe this book, however fantastic, would help him get more familiar with it. Already he felt like paying more attention when Mother might say things about the woods. He looked around again on the moony richness of it. He did, however, know something about its shadows. He had been through these woods in all kinds of light and had never got turned around in them.

He had also been through his own young life in all kinds of dark and light and, if he got turned around in it occasionally, he always found his way back out into what was recognizable as wholesome and good and right. You don't live in all kinds of weather very long before you can recognize a healthy atmosphere. ...And he did not think conditions right in the truck camper they were calling home. Not anymore. There just wasn't enough room in there to contain a blow. He closed the book and walked on.

~~~~~~~~~~~

Below the moon-struck triple summit of Blackwell Mountain juts Buck Hill, with its burned out clearing and the truck camper housing the Twitchell-Prince union. Peter Prince climbed out of the camper and walked across to the cellar hole full of charred timbers. He was going to go nuts if he had to stay in there much longer. Place wasn't big enough for a gnat's ass.

He dug in his crumpled pack of Viceroys, pulled out a half flattened cigarette and lit it. Peter Prince drew deeply and exhaled, watching the smoke drift out into the bright night. He looked right off across the valley toward great Jasper Mountain, the Gott'im town mountain, domed and shining in the night. The murmur of Nathan's voice jabbering away sounded almost pleasant from here. Peter was glad to be removed from its proximity, let the beauty of the night absorb it.

How that kid can talk so much when he's poring over the homework, that stubble of pencil gripped tight in his grubby hand as it spurted across the page. And Benaiah—always scowling and letting his little brother get to him. If they fought one more time he was going to clobber them for sure. Either that or Chrischana. And he knew where that would lead. Daniel does right to get out of here every night. ... He must be doing his homework at school, or the library. Kid gets good grades.

He looked down into the wide pit at his feet, at the moonlight gleaming off charred bubbles of the Twitchell farmhouse timbers.

He thought of the vandals who had destroyed the abandoned and rotting farmhouse. Probably partying, and, who knows, maybe they didn't mean to do it. Things happen when you're having a good time.... Which I'm not. *Not now*.

It was getting harder to tell if any of them were having a good time now that sugaring-off was over. It's crazy to live like this ... and there's so much work to be done. The Town was not going to allow them to continue either, so they had to apply for permits and build another house and drill a new well and put in a septic system and.... Chrischana wants to plant trees! An orchard for crying out loud. They'd had a great life in Phoenix where he was a motorcycle mechanic just about set to go into business for himself—and she had to throw in the monkey wrench by coming back to this place to do these kinds of things.

And to get away from you, he reminded himself. Yeah, Hermann would like that. Maybe you ought to keep reminding yourself, Peter, since you're so apt to forget. Remind yourself of her mildness and patience, firmness and toughness. (No Hermann, don't remind myself of my dissatisfaction, even my despair.)

Peter kept steadily dragging on his cigarette until it went out and then he lit another off it, tossing the butt into the cellar hole.

The wind seems to be shifting, the smoke drifting back now into his eyes. He moves along to one side of the pit. "You don't want to do the work," his counselor, Hermann Gottesman, keeps reminding him.

Well, Hermann, you try doing it. You're sitting there in Jericho doing exactly what you want with your books and your *Kids Cafe* and your substance abuse counseling. You're doing your work and it all seems pretty manageable and you don't feel hopeless but I feel hopeless. I'll tell you what won't work. *This* won't work. Be honest, be honest. How goddamn honest do you want me to be. *This* is honest, Hermann.

He looked bitterly over at the beat-up camper, the glow of gaslight within faint and somehow romantic. Weather was coming, he saw, from the direction of Gottheim. It would probably move up the mountain and maybe even engulf them. It had done this before. The moon still gleamed off the fenders of his Harley beside the camper in front of Chrischana's new secondhand truck. He ought to go to the utility shed and get out his bike cover—keep the acid-soot from that goddamn tire fire off its leather and finish.

But he stood there, smoking.

He heard the camper door open, Nathan's jabbering still going, louder; saw his common-law wife climb out, her long braid swinging off her shoulder. She looked off toward Gottheim. She looked back at him. She went over to the beat-up metal shed and he saw the play of the flashlight beam as she rummaged in there and came out with the cover. Did she have ESP? Did he have her trained? Or was she just too good for him? He thought these thoughts bitterly. She's always got to make me feel guilty.

She covered the bike and came over to him, saying, "They'll be done soon." She stood by him and he looked at her face in the moonlight. It was calm and full, with the slightly exotic Native American features that came to her through her mother. He scarcely noticed, so full was he of recrimination. She stepped back, seeming to sense it.

Chrischana looked off again in the direction of Gottheim.

"Don't tell me you sensed a change in the weather?" He said with a nod toward the bike.

She merely nodded. This minimizing was a shelter she went into when she felt a change in his mood.

She was silent, looking back at the camper. They heard Nathan emit a loud "*Ow!*" They both knew it was bound to escalate, this provocation, this tit-for-tat.

The breeze was strengthening and again she looked in the direction of Gottheim and the view of approaching weather now dimming the mountain slopes and woodland out across from them. "Daniel's still out," she said without looking at him. The moon behind him still shone and he saw the contour of her full cheeks and high cheekbones and lashes, turned away from him. "Maybe I should go look fah'em."

She waited.

"Yeah?"

The faint sneer in his voice reached into her, and she said nothing.

Then he relented and said, sulking, "I'll go."

He moved past her toward the cycle. It was in her mouth to suggest that he walk down in case Daniel was coming up through the woods some way other than the dirt road. Without the bike they'd hear one another, maybe. She watched as he removed the cover, restraining everything pushing out to speak through her.

But the camper was erupting in squabbles and the Harley already exploding to life beside it. He wheeled around and without even a nod in her direction, took off through the thickets bordering the track on either side.

Just as well, she thought. He better get out of here. But the thought of Daniel came back to her. They are going to miss one another, sure. She chewed a bit on her lower lip.... He'll find his way back.... They both will. She walked back to the camper and peered inside, saying, "Quit fighting and get into bed! It's too late fah anathin else now. And shut down that light."

Nathan started protesting and she shut the door on him. If that light wasn't out in two minutes he'd be sorry and he knew it. Chrischana walked back to the cellarhole to look out at the weather coming as a black mist, dissolving her view of the Meguntics as it came on from the direction of Quaker and Gottheim. Ceylon Segar's tire fire was still mingling its toxic vapors with the weather of the mountains after all these weeks. When would they get that thing extinguished and make the place livable again? When would the asthmatics and others with breathing problems, the old, be able to stop suffering? Bronchitis, sinusitis, depression, sadness. Stuff was in all the houses, curtains, carpets, floorboards, couches, air ducts. When would the woodland be safe from its fires? They better get that thing taken care of before the dry season gets here. All they needed to complete the devastation were underground fires, fire leaping from root to root, pine pitch burning, exploding out the tops of trees ....

She was starting to rage herself—and no Harley to roar off on either.

Still gazing out there, she murmured, "Why don't *You* do something?"

It's work, I know. You've got work to do, I've got work to do. All God's children got work to do. It was a thought halfway between bitter and flippant, but she let it go. She wasn't going to be like Petey.

She looked over at the camper. It was dark. It even seemed quiet. "Thank you," she said still looking at it. She could see the metal of its frame gleaming in moonlight. She smiled. She could actually back the truck up under there and haul the thing away, if she wanted to. She could do it while Peter was at work. Should. Before he starts on me again.

....You could go insane.

But God wouldn't like it. He doesn't like the tire fire either. He doesn't like the flabby system that unleashed it. She sighed and went back to the camper. She would tuck them in and open her own bed. Hers and Peter's. But she would not sleep.

Chrischana Twitchell lay a long time thinking and looking up through the narrow jalousie-glass at the bright sky. She lay planning the heirloom orchard, turning over in her mind the various varieties, considering what to choose. Baldwins were good winter keepers but the Westfield-seek-no-further and the Northern Spy had narrower crowns requiring less space. She liked their names.

Then the sky darkened. She heard the pinging of soot on metal, and she could no longer restrain her real thoughts pushing to speak through her. It was dark as pitch inside the camper. She thought the phrase apt. Daniel would like it. The even breathing of her other two sons reassured her. So. Still dressed in shirt and jeans and the jacket she had worn to alert Peter, Chrischana climbed back out into the night. A world and night so different from its beginning as to be a discredit to its Creator. Yes, she thought, standing there in a baptism of soot and acid mist, You've got work. Looks like Your day of rest is ovah.

She flicked on the flashlight to find the reach of its beam quenched in the drizzling dark mist, reflecting it. Nevermind. She would feel her way down the mountain. She would call Daniel. It couldn't quench the sound of her prayers.

~~~~~~~~~~

Peter Prince had wound down through moonlight still streaming with leafless tree shadows; down, down on stretches of the mountain road deep in the shadow of conifer. His stepson Daniel was so deep in the woods that he had not heard the far-off purring of the Harley as it drifted down behind a distant shoulder of the mountain. Peter watched along the road, expecting to see the dark shape of Daniel at any moment in the beam of his headlamp. But he was thinking, Why am I supposed to be doing what *she* wants? An orchard!

Peter chewed over such thoughts all the way down the side of the mountain until he slid neatly out into the wide light of the moon on the Lower Intervale Road. It seemed to him that he had been chewing on these things and swallowing and regurgitating and chewing again ever since they moved out of the apartment in Gottheim, when the roads were clear again.

On the smooth white road he was tempted to ramp it up but thought he had better keep the pace if he wasn't going to miss Daniel.

Daniel would make it back all right, but would *he*? God! It was so tempting to turn the bike around and float off into the night on the back road to Guildford!

He could always save himself at the last minute by turning off to Jericho and flopping down on Hermann's beat up old couch. The obese giant was always ready to listen to him .... Though he could get disgusted, Peter remembered wryly.

He remembered the story Gottesman had told him that time in Jericho when the power was off. About how far he had had to fall, how deep, in order to climb back up again—Hermann Gottesman. Clearly he was trying to scare me! Well it won't work, Hermann. You can scare infants into behaving well but you can't help full-grown men that way. It's got to come from something more genuine than fear and trembling. Go back to the counseling books and learn how to help me, for God's sake. And please don't bring up the "necessary" work again. I need relief, not more pressure.

~~~~~~~~~~~

The night of Hermann's story had been cloudy and dim but lit by a few neon signs. He had swung off his bike on Main Street in Jericho, stepped across the sidewalk and up the stoop. The cool elegance of "Kind of Blue" came drifting out of Hermann Gottesman's *Kids Cafe*. He had just stepped over the threshold when darkness overcame him. The horn trailed on a long deflating note and stopped. He looked down the street and saw darkness and a few dim shapes of buildings.

"You in there, Hermann?"

The voice characteristically treble and soft came to him. "C'mon in Prince." It still amazed him that such a big man could speak with such a small voice. "It's dark on the street, I suppose?"

Peter came in, his hand on the loose old doorknob, feeling his way with his feet. He felt for the pool table and let it guide him to the couch where he knew Hermann would be sitting, probably holding onto a full liter of Coke with his huge dimpled fleshy hand. "Kids all got somewhere else to be tonight, Hermann?" The silence of the whole town seemed invoked by the dark. Then a set of headlights brightened the street, passing, and another.

"No. I told them to leave."

"But it's early, ain't it. We weren't supposed to get down to work for another half hour."

"I told them to leave."

He heard Hermann take a swig from the plastic bottle. Prince found the ratty old chair beside the couch and sank into it. He could feel the bare greasy spots of its arms where the wool had worn off from years of use. "I'm not deaf, Hermann. Why did you tell them to leave?"

"... I knew it was going to get dark."

"So you're a prophet now." He thought, if I was Jewish like you, I would've put a question mark on the end of that. "My eyes aren't adjusting ... or it's *really* dark. Maybe beavers took down a tree across a power line, like they did in Gott'im that time." There's something spooky about this. *Hermann* is spooky tonight.

"What've you been doing, Peter?"

"Not drinking, Herr Mentor." But he knew he was not going to jostle Hermann out of this. "Not drinking, Hermann."

"But you will be, Peter."

"So you *are* a prophet now, Hermann?"

There was silence. There was darkness.

"Did I ever tell you how far it took me?"

Peter was silent sitting in the dark. He would welcome the sound of the refrigerator coming back on, the music beginning again. The occasional beams passed out on the street, visible through the streaked plate glass. There were some barely discernible shapes now in the long narrow room. Some sort of texture to the interior darkness. He fumbled in a shirt pocket for cigarettes, found his lighter in the pocket of his jeans. He lit up and the yellow flare showed forth the room and Hermann's great bespeckled dark solemn eyes on him, as though they had been there all the time in the dark and seeing Peter as though it were day. He snapped the lighter shut and shoved it back into his pocket. He drew on the cigarette. Prince exhaled the invisible smoke, but it was as though he had not even touched that nicotine craving nor tasted the cigarette.

He resigned himself. "Maybe you better tell me, then."

And Hermann Gottesman had begun by telling him the story of his plan for the long sabbatical to write that great philosophical/psychological treatise. He had decided to head for the coast of Maine first for a little rest and relaxation away from his friends who meant so well. And away from his two drinking buddies who maybe meant not so well, but he had to get away from them anyway. Because that's all they were: drinking buddies. There was nothing else going on, intellectually, emotionally, or otherwise. Worse, what was left of his family were urging the observances on him as a duty to the memory of the gassed and burned. And he had never seen the coast of Maine.

He found himself in Guildford at that old hotel down by the tracks.

Peter had been incredulous at this: Guildford is almost two hundred miles by winding roads from the coast, smack in the mountains surrounded by woods. But he spoke no sign; Hermann was ongoing with the tale.

He finds himself, next, standing on the bridge spanning the river and staring out at the hellish glow of the paper mill, its pink vapor lights playing off steam rolling in great sheets and billows off the driers and into the night-dark miasma of the Guildford/Spain valley air. The glow even plays off the rapids churning, tumbling and foaming with hellish spite among the rocks in the river far below. He is standing here thinking, Wasn't I going to be on the Gulf of Maine?—Casco Bay?

Fearful, Gottesman went back to the bar in the barren hotel to continue drinking. Then he must've gone up to his room to lie down because that's where he woke and heard it again. The same voice he heard while standing on the bridge. The one that earlier spoke each word distinctly, scaring him back into the bar.

"*You .. have.. left .. your.. friend. . to. . burn.. in .. the. . house.*" Each word is spoken as though it is the only word, by a calm voice right beside him. "*The . . officers .. are.. looking.. for . . you.*" Hermann sits up and looks about him but, as on the bridge, there is no one. Yet he begins to consider: the voice is kind, maybe it's true. Maybe it happened. Maybe I don't remember it. He thrills with fear.

"Follow me. I will help you."

It must be an illusion. I'm going insane. I will distrust it. But, thrilling, he jumps from the bed and goes to the windows staring out at the pink glowing sky over the rooftops of Guildford. Again the voice says, "Follow .. me, I .. will ..help .. you .. escape."

"It was a hoarse kindly voice, Prince. Something of a whisper; but not particularly ghostly. That of a friend. I did follow it in the dark, out of the room, along the hall, down the stairs, to the lobby, and then into the kitchen where there was a door. By light thrown in from the alley window I saw that it was a dark paneled door. It had a rattling knob, and following the voice I turned that handle and there were more stairs, going down."

Then two turns and Hermann stands in the darkness at the bottom of the stairs, trying to feel his way with his hands; the kindly firm voice attending him: "Follow me."

But he cannot quite trust. He feels with his feet, finds a stair to mount, feels for the second stair but it is empty space. Gently he kneels his great weight down upon the basement floor and feels with his hand. The dankness of a well comes up into his face and nostrils, speaking through cold water about how far Hermann Gottesman had been taken by it.

~~~~~~~~~~~~

The house, with its semicircular drive, seemed more or less a museum, a three-story mansion with mansard roof and dormers. Complete with cupola and gilded weather vane; painted paneling, columns, piazzas with balustrades, even porte-cochere side entrance. Rhetta Bearce was walking around the dormant gardens of what some people in Gottheim referred to as the mansion, as yet the only one for miles around. It had always been so. Until the Harry and Julius Goldings' ... what would you call it?—extravaganza?—*rustic* extravaganza-in-progress.

Well, she thought, it had *been* in progress before all those tires caught fire. The ski business being interrupted, they've all taken off and are waiting elsewhere for the soot to settle.

It was late but at last the horrible atmosphere was lifting. She had seen the bright disk of the moon shining through and decided it was time to come out and touch up the mulch and maybe refurbish the landscape fabric for one or two of the beds. Of course there would be another month at least of night frosts but she thought the dangers were over for the perennials she had put in last October. She got down on her knees and began piling together the wet soot-covered straw of that corner where she had neglected use of the fabric.

Wearing one of Lyman's old woolen shirts Rhetta gathered an armload to her broad but aging bosom and took it off to the compost heap. She dumped it into the first bin and thought, *Better go get the wheelbarrow.* She was about to go to the shed behind the summer house when she looked up at the moon and saw that it was almost clear. Everything she looked upon was coming cleaner in its light. She looked off down toward the village, but could barely perceive a glow in that direction. Oh well. The weather is taking itself off from here, anyway.

... Wonder where Lyman is?

He has possibly managed to avoid the terrible brew that Ceylon Segar has cooked up for us here in the valley today ... if he went off to one or another of his far-flung tree farms, possibly that tract up in Somerset County. It may be raining up there but she doubted it would be sooting. He never has trouble avoiding the discomfiting. ...But to be fair he won't hesitate to confront it in his interest either.

Why should she worry? Lyman was as hardened as a bag of old rocks. If anybody could take care of himself it was Lyman Bearce: He had seen to it that every one of his enemies had been taken care of. ... All but that new one, what did they call him, Liquidation Leonard? ... And then there was poor little Theodora Prescott. She almost chuckled over her husband's failure there. The town scatterbrain, as he referred to the girl, had done something no one would have foreseen —in giving the chair factory to the employees. He had not got over that yet! (Neither had Theo's fiancee, James Fay.) She almost smiled.

... And yet she was worried. Rhetta Bearce could not really put her finger on it, but she had lived with Bearce long enough to ... to know him. And what she was seeing now she did not quite know. There was something new, but what was it? She had not even been aware of any difference, she was sure—not consciously anyway— until now in these thoughts. As she removed the rocks from its corners and tugged away at the fabric shielding clumps of ornamental grasses, she thought, This is going to be more work than I wanted just now.

She raised herself slowly from stooping, a hand to the small of her back, releasing a soft puff of air. Well! That's enough of that. And she thought, staring off towards Gottheim again, *It's enough of those strange thoughts about Lyman, as well.* He's no different, and I'm not going to start looking at him differently now. Wouldn't it be sweet if I started in on mothering the old bag of rocks after all these years of wrangling with him? Neither of us needs that!

Lyman Bearce needing a mother!? She laughed out loud, she almost cackled. She could not begin to picture Bearce being mothered, being six years old, in any need of TLC, in need of ... of anything whatever. It's absurd! He was the kind of man that wouldn't tell you if his leg was broken. The kind of man who wouldn't mention it if he fell down three flights of stairs. If he had Alzheimer's you wouldn't know it. He was the kind of man who would be walking around the woods barking orders on his two-way three weeks after he was dead—and no one would know it. It's absurd!

A very strange image of her husband's bones, a skeleton walking beneath tall woods—a two-way radio to his grinning teeth—came into her mind. Suddenly shivering, she backed away from the shadows of blue spruce by the drive where she had set monkshood and European ginger last year. Then she heard it. Distantly.

She would have sworn there were horses on the other side of the hill, coming up the road out of Gottheim and driven at an alarming rate, screaming and neighing and snorting. How very strange. No.... It wasn't that way but over there, far more distant, as though from the top of Jasper Mountain or way over in Madrid or some place. Rhetta Bearce turned around and saw a team of wild Belgians barreling straight toward her on that curve of the drive smack in front of the house. With a great box of a carriage overshadowing—it was huge, it was monstrous, it was going to run her over!

But at the last moment it swerved aside, keeping with the curve, heading back out toward the road. Looking stunned at the squared back of the box carriage with its sidelights and wheels flinging gravel, disappearing through the grove by the road, she heard distinctly these distant words:

Haw, haw, lay'em away! Lay'em away, my townswoman!

Rhetta Bearce had stumbled backward into the trees, the spruces upholding and cradling her. Now she tumbled to her feet and into the white gravel of the drive, staring in the direction of that passing apparition. Yes, it was gone. It had probably never been there to begin with. Rhetta held out her trembling hand and stared at it. *Me, trembling.*

Dazed and distracted, she started in the direction of its vanishment without any thought for the reality of the thing. Without any thought for her movements stepping deliberately toward the darkness at the end of the drive. She was thinking instead, very carefully, about how she was never going to mention this to anybody, about how she was going to hope fervently for the rest of her life that she never saw or heard anything like again. And she thought carefully about how she understood it all now:

Lyman is all right. There is nothing different about Lyman Bearce. It's you there's something wrong with! It's you... — all wrong!

~~~~~~~~~

She was standing in the shade of the trees staring vacantly out on the white road in the moonlight. There came the cracking of a twig behind. Rhetta Bearce emitted a shriek. She hopped. She looked backward, gaping and wild, wide-eyed, on Elda Simon coming white and kerchiefed out of the trees. In the light of the moon she was ghostly, her clothing looked white, all but her pale sneakers and jeans.

"Elda Simon—! You scared the jee-*zus* out'o me. What ah you doing way ovah heah in the dark?!" And it was out of her mouth before she knew it. "—You didn't see—anything." She went quiet, looking off toward the direction of the village.

The slight woman peers at her, shyly smiling. Even in her distraction Rhetta Bearce notes, with her habitual surprise over the fact, the grin is like that of Elda's son Balder Simon.

"I saw ... something." It was a small speech, and Elda Simon is also silent now.

"Elda ... did you—what did you see?" And Rhetta thinks, in my own way I'm as bad as Bearce. Elda persists in silence, and she decides to wait her out.

Ask yourself, say I, the hermit who lives on Crazy Knoll. Are things always what you think they are? Are you what you think you are? Are people what you are thinking of them? Do you know what is happening in the cells of the membrane lining your colon right now? Do you know what is working its way toward you through the air as you read these words? I am ninety-three years old, and I might answer yes to the last question. I'd be very surprised if I knew anything else for sure. However I do know the answer to the first three questions: The answer to the first three questions is no. Elda would not know the answers either.

You may or may not know about Elda Simon's macular degeneration. (Nevertheless there are times when she can see better in the dark than in daylight. It has something to do with the difference between the cones and rods of the retina, the kind of light available, and what she is looking at. She has adapted to accommodate her perambulations.) Contrary to what Rhetta was thinking, she was not hesitant to admit she had seen an apparition: Elda was hesitant to admit that she had not been able to see it *clearly*.

Well, thinks Rhetta, *If you're not going to mention it, neither am I.*

Elda is looking off down the road but then she turns and says, "What I don't understand is the steam. Theya was vapor pouring out of their nostrils, even the driver's. ... Like 'twas the middle of wintah. In't so cold as all that now."

Relief fills Rhetta, but she says merely, "...Yes ... I hadn't noticed that detail then, but now that you mention it .... "

Again they are silent, speculatively.

Rhetta said, "But what was it, do you think? It wasn't a carriage—not really.... It had columns and panels, maybe carved drapery with a glass window in the center. It went by so fast I didn't think I'd remember such detail ... I don't think I even noticed then."

Elda was silent.

"Something antique, of course, but beautifully preserved. The driver even looked ... well, antique. He was bundled up, but still there was something antique about him. Maybe it was the bowler."

Elda said nothing. We don't know that much about Elda anymore. No one would know what she was doing out there that night. Likely some errand: There was that pack on her back.

Rhetta ventured, "... I *heard* something. Did you?"

" ...Sounded like 'twas further 'way."

This lacked the kind of detail Rhetta Bearce was after. "I heard a voice way off in the distance."

Elda nodded.

Rhetta was ready to give up, but then she said, "Wondah what he meant by it?"

Elda said she did not know.

"I almost think I saw some scrollwork or something arabesque. Maybe leaves or flowers ... something."

Elda was silent.

It was that unwieldy moment when one or the other would start with the excuses; time for some awkward verbal device used when either, having nothing to say, said (in essence), we will part now. What more could be said about it? But who would want to replay the apparition again alone in thought—which was surely what would occur if they parted now.

"... Have you ever noticed how many flowers, flower parts, look male?" wondered Elda aloud.

"Oh yes. I notice it especially in the roadside wildflowers: mullein, plantain, not to mention lady-slippers, which look like gonads to me."

"And then there are the bugbanes in the woods."

"Pickerelweed in the ponds, and white bog orchis in the bogs."

What in the State of Maine are we doing? Rhetta wondered as they stood in conversation. ...Standing here in the dark talking about similarities between plants and male sex organs. It's crazy. The whole night from beginning to end. Absurd.

~~~~~~~~~

> *The Naiad was intimately connected to her body of water and her very existence seems to have depended on it. If a stream dried up, its Naiad expired. The waters over which Naiades presided were thought to be endowed with inspirational, medicinal, or prophetic powers. Thus the Naiades were frequently worshipped by the ancient Greeks in association with divinities of healing, fertility and growth.* —Bulfinch's Mythology

Approaching over the rutted road with Balder Simon in his patched pickup Gloria Fay saw the glimmer of golden lights through the tree stems. It was the opening season for gathering smelts. It was also the season when smelts gathered one another in fertility. The night air was cool but they were traveling slow over the ruts the windows were down. It would be maybe more than a month before the bugs showed. But the ice was out now and smelts were running. Gloria was happier than anything, being out like this in the mysterious night with her boyfriend Balder.

They passed a gap in the trees near shore and she looked out upon the wide dark pond, its shoreline half-strung with the gems of the lanterns of fishermen out with their great nets after the smelts. The lights shone above and below the encircling shoreline, reflecting. "You know what this reminds me of?"

"Something pagan?" His answer was fast on the heels of her query and she saw the flash of a grin he aimed at her before turning back to the sight himself. "Something about the equinox or the Maypole or Easter."

She jabbed him in the arm with her fist. "How'd you know about Easter?"

"I d'know. Just a lucky guess. I told you about my grandmother. All that information passes through the placenta from generation to generation."

"I guess that explains why I have to read up on the stuff if I want to learn anything. It seems everything that crossed my placenta's all Baptist related." She smiled.

"I wouldn't be so quick t' get rid o'that stuff if I was you. What do you want to go and be a pagan for, anyway?"

"Somebody's got to undo all the hardship placed on us by Christianity."

"Like having all our sins took away? What hardship you talkin' bout? Seems to me you've had it pretty good with all that you was raised with, master's degrees, two homes and brand new skis every year." He flashed her another grin.

"You know what I mean—psychological hardship. All the guilt trips, and having to do everything just so or lose God's favor ... go to hell, stuff like that." It was her turn to grin. "Besides, I don't see you going to church."

"I would." He looked at her, grinning more. "If I could stand it."

"Hah! See, we are agreed."

He looked over at glorious Glory's even features, shadowed in the cab of the truck, but her sleek blond pageboy still held its light. He wanted to say, *But that's about all we ah agreed on.* Then, slowly, he did say it. Balder gave a slow smile.

On the last curve the track had turned away from the lights and they were in the moony shaded woodland, Gloria staring out the window upon the mysterious crosshatching of shadows. They were deep in the woods several miles from Gottheim and on what was possibly one of the best dates of her life. She sighed. It was true about their disagreements: she was a confirmed consumer, he a traditionalist. She bought everything; he made and repaired things, was going to start growing his food. He wanted children. She... didn't think so… didn't know.

He turned his attention to the track in his high beams but picked up the thread of the conversation again. "So you ah throwing out what you call the mahden tradition with all its hyper industrial support—I guess I take back what I said, we do agree on something else. But with that pagan stuff you still got gods getting mad and needing propitiation n'manipulations and all that stuff. Plus, you don't know who your friends ah. Who's the Lord Jesus if not that?"

"Well, he should not have let himself get attached to all that other stuff, that's all."

"How many masters' degrees d'you say you had?"

"—Just the one," she said dryly. But then she could not resist adding, "And I'm going to go after another one in classical Greek literature, too, if I can."

The track had widened out and the truck's beams revealed either side lined with pickups and old Broncos, a new Blazer or two. They got out and he reached in back for the gear: a propane lantern, long green waders, the great smelt net. He handed her a cooking pot: "Handy place to put 'em once theya caught! L'me get these on, and we'll just go get'em."

"Aren't they just a teeny bit ridiculous?" She couldn't help but arch an eyebrow over the waders.

Balder loved it when she did that. "I'll be the envy of evah body theya! Ones without will all be losing their legs fah I do, n'hev to give up fore they get their two quarts."

He shrugged into the suspenders, grinning as big and bright as the lantern he had lit. She burst out laughing.

"You look like a blond, black-bearded frog from outer space—after it's jumped! Oh Balder, you should see yourself!"

"I'm seeing myself right now." He indicated her ridicule with a gesture. He might have said that he wanted to go on seeing it for the rest of his life. He did not say it. Balder Simon did not think he needed to.

They followed over a beaten uneven path, the light of their propane lantern moving through the woods between them, seething. After passing a few others coming or going, Balder said he wanted to see the brook black with smelts.

"But aren't smelts silver? I saw some in the fish display at the supermarket."

"Black just means packed with smelts."

They came to the stream and he shone the lantern onto the excited milling strands of mating life. They reminded her of water weeds drifting in the current. Balder walked on, the great net on a long pole projecting off his shoulder. She caught up with him. "Aren't you going to get the smelt?"

"We don't dip the brook. Wouldn't be fair, gettin'em while theya in the act. You got to get 'em in the pond where they circle round its outer edges. Wouldn't be none left fah us if we dip where they drop n'fertilize their eggs. See, they'll be looking fah that stream n'then we'll get 'em when they go past us on the shore. You'll be on the shore. I'll be in the water. Those lights all round the pond is like a lure to the fish when they school past. Here, turn that down a dite. This looks like a good spot."

She lowered the flame, stood on one rock staring down into the water. He waded between rocks with a net and submerged it. Her eyes were still dark from the light of the lantern, but sensing Balder's suppressed excitement, she looked harder. Then she exclaimed in a fervent whisper: "There!!" But he had already seen and was lifting the net, fish wriggling in the bottom. Popping like corn. He grabbed a fistful and tossed them into the pot she held out to him. She watched him lay the net on the water and let it settle where, edging the shallows, flecks of lights flickered through the waters. Now he dipped again and lifted against the drag. He stuck in his hand and threw her another fistful. Each time he lifted she watched his muscles flex before allowing her eye to be drawn back to the fish.

Gloria Fay was wholly alive, coming out after a long long winter and a cold, ash-strewn spring. All her dreams for earning a living by investment and wit in Gottheim had been covered in smoke and ash, but now she was alive again. And here with Balder in the water again, this time in the pond not far from some mountain stream pouring out into the wide experience of moon-gleaming life. He held out the net to her, she plunged her hand into the cold squirming fishes, she popped them into the pot.

They were sitting on shore under the shadows, resting even as some of the lights began to dim and move away into the trees. There was cold lake water covering the fish in the pot where they still moved, but sluggishly. Gloria leaned against Balder, dreamily, happy in the reflected gleam of the water, now that Balder's lantern was out.

Balder was going to say something, she thought. Yes, Balder spoke.

"Since you stotted mooning ovah Jaspa Mountain like it was some sort o'deity ... and since I'm named fah that there Norse god y'studied, when ah you going to stot worshiping me?"

Gloria said nothing. It was going to take her a moment to come up with it. Then,

"...God of gladness and light, meet Gloria Fay. She is a naiad."

"And when I did look around, there on the bridge, within a few paces of me, a huge black dog was sitting, with the face of a man—a human face, if ever I saw one, turned full up to the moonlight. It remained just long enough to give me a clear view of it, and then vanished; and ever since, when I think of Satan, I call to mind the dog-man on the bridge." —Supernaturalism of New England, John Greenleaf Whittier

Prone, fifteen-year-old Cindabilla lifted a heavy head at the sound of an engine purring past. She tried to focus her eyes on the moving object – maybe a motorcycle. She thought she saw the gleam of something but couldn't be sure. Cindabilla rolled over and glanced up at the moon, seeing its circle through a thick shroud. There were two of them—two moons. She tried to move again. She felt a groan or maybe an upchuck coming on but decided to keep still in case the engine was something she didn't want to face. She was finding that it wasn't too comfortable lying here in the roots or rocks or whatever it was on the shore of the Old Ferry Landing. Then she was on her elbow, quietly vomiting.

She lay back on a sharp rock then moved aside a little, trying to nestle down into the earth. *Ah ... feels better ....* But the two moons were still whirling.... She sat up, leaning against a big rock. *Oh, why dint I listen to Daniel Twitchell?* Cindabilla considered taking off his jacket and throwing herself into the filthy river. *That'll get me out of this.* But she sat there. The moon faded into the dirty mist.

The engine, she noticed, had stopped. She looked over her shoulder to see a form walking near the fire pit, embers still giving off a faint glow. What was it doing?

The dark someone stooped and came up with something in its hand. She saw it was a man, someone she was familiar with. ...Daniel's stepfather .... Probably came to give him a lift home— way too late. He was holding up one of the bottles and shaking it. She heard it clink as he threw it back down and picked up another. She wanted to say, What are you doing, why don't you listen to Daniel? But her mouth didn't feel like speaking, her body didn't feel like moving. Petey Prince? Ah you going to get like Uncle Ferddy again? Are you going to turn everything inside out and make Daniel go away fom me?

Peter Prince put the bottle to his lips and drank what was left of it straight down. Then he went rummaging through the other bottles, and the case clinking with empties. She heard him swearing. He held up a bottle but then he stopped.

They both felt it.

A sudden yet vague sensation of horror, welling up like an intuition.

They both heard it. A muted growling, a snarling, a snapping. As though from a hundred. The sound came from far away but when they both looked toward it they saw something on a rock by the misty dim shore. It was only a few feet from Petey and as large as Uncle Ferddy's wolf-dog. But it had the face of a man. Oh yes, they saw. It was the face of a man. Staring at them.

No one said anything, not Cindabilla, not Petey, not the dog-man. A great Presence of Evil, and loathing and madness enveloped them almost to bursting. Cindabilla thought it was more than anything she could bear. *"Daniel!!"* she screamed. *"Daniel!!"*

And then it was gone. And all the hatred and loathing and cursing and damnation had gone off with it.

But now the storm had come on.

~~~~~~~~

At first it is nothing but a vague mist, scarcely discernible from any midnight mist on a seeming all but moonless night. All is suffused in clammy darkness. It's a netherworld. You are not yet divorced from your surroundings of vague dissolving shapes. You look at your hand held out with a certain sense that it is your hand. Somehow you can tell if anything big is blocking your way. You move around it with a faint sense of reality. But that sense is rapidly slipping, dissolving like everything else in the darkness of night and ashen mist surrounding you.

There's weather, drizzling a strange mixture of moisture and metal and what seems pumice or talc. You can't see to say what it is but it gives you a feeling of all this. If it were not for the drizzle driving it downward you wouldn't be able to breathe. It is not a driving rain even so. It's more nebulous than that, creating a world within a world unlike that first or outer world. You are alone there. It seeming only you. There is nothing but you and the panicking atmosphere you inhabit. You cannot really differentiate between the two. It is a oneness of almost uncreated being, frightful and reft of innocence.

The spiritual horror that overcame the representatives of two generations had vanished with Cindabilla's fierce cry after Daniel. Following the vacuum of his initial relief, to Peter Prince it seemed a cry *for* Daniel, his son. He looked at the bottle he still held in his hand and could barely see it. He threw it down in disgust. Self disgust. Self-loathing came over him but he said merely, "That you, Cindabilla? Where is he?"

"Didn't you see that shit-awful thing!!?" she screeched.

He could just barely see her skinny shade stumble up and weave through the rocks toward him. At first he answered nothing but then he said, "To tell you the truth I'm glad to hear you say it. Thought I was seeing things, feeling things."

"Asshole, we *were* seeing and feeling things!"

It was Cindabilla, after all, and he could see that she was drunk. She did not regularly call him an asshole so he let it go by.

Perceiving her start up the lane he called after her, "Where's Daniel?!"

But Cindabilla made no answer. Recollection of the thing came back into his mind and he shuddered involuntarily. Worse, Cindabilla was already gone, leaving him alone with —it. He found his bike and climbed on, kicking up the stand, igniting it. He tried the high beam then lowered it and started feeling his way up from the river, looking for her. Was that Daniel's leather jacket she was wearing?

He tried the length of the lane slowly all the way back to the Lower Intervale Road, calling her as he went. He didn't think it was possible to be any darker than it had been by the shore but it was in this tunnel of firs, with that sinister ash-falling mist. It was definitely falling now, and no longer merely an atmosphere.

Though he went calling for Cindabilla, his thoughts were on Daniel and he realized that his stepson had been gone from the landing and the party a long time. Peter had been attracted to the site on seeing a car full of drunken joyriders depart out the Landing Road. He cursed himself impotently for seven kinds of fool in having started off on the bike in the first place. No doubt Daniel had come through the woods and the puckerbrush. Either that, or he had just missed him some other way, some way that he could not think of now. The dog-man with its hundreds still snarling distantly through his thoughts, Peter Prince decided to go back down the Lower Intervale Road and find his way again up to the camper on Blackwell Mountain. Possibly Daniel, whom he felt for as his own son, was home safe again. Concern for his safety kept the panic at bay. Cinda was something else, but if she was anything it was tough, and he was not going to worry about her. She never seemed to worry about herself.

~~~~~~~~~~~~~~~~~

Cindabilla is many chilly wet miles from home. Cindabilla is drunk. Cindabilla is staggering along the lane in a thick darkness. She has been scared by something that lingers, powerfully.

If only the dog-man would get out of her head. If only the darkness would get of her eyes. If only Ceylon Segar's tires would stop falling. It feels like they're falling straight on her head without being burnt up first. No, it feels like she's wearing the whole tire dump on her head. Cindabilla wobbles a bit, she giggles. ...Ohhh, Daniel. Oh Daniel.

"... Didn't theya used to be ... wasn't theya an ol'
tumbledown on the field lane through th'woods? ... Old field lane ...
old field lane .... Corn down by th'river?"

She had been walking roughly the middle of the lane but
now she teetered to the shoulder, trying to feel for an intersection she
remembered seeing on the way down. She heard the cycle coming
up on its way toward the Lower Intervale Road and, looking over her
shoulder, saw the dark misted light of its beam passing into the
woods on a curve. She almost fell over. Cindabilla let herself fall
hidden into the woods, just as the beam went ghosting past. She
couldn't believe it: Peter Prince was still calling her. He's an
asshole, she thought, but I wish I'd a father like'um.

She rose on her elbow and puked again. Then she felt
better. Maybe that was the intersection she glimpsed in the beam of
his headlamp a moment ago—or was it an hour? She was lying on
her back in the damp shoulder full of seedlings. She climbed to her
feet and wobbled on. (Cindabilla finds the shed and goes in to sleep
away the filthy storm.)

~~~~~~~~~~~~

On a lower flank of Jasper Mountain the paths of two men are about
to converge. Lyman Bearce has let his obsession overpower his
usually canny common sense, that which has contributed much to
his sound forestry and business practices. In the moments when
Cindabilla looks up to see two dimly circled moons in the dark of
developing weather, Bearce is coolly searching for the mysterious
new road he saw from the other side of the river, slowly nosing his
Blazer up the only deadend that the road could have been cut from.
...Unless ... could it have been cut into that knoll and upward —
beyond the backside of the gravel pit?

The mist has not yet begun to fall when he sees lights in the
rearview. Who-the-hell...? Well, maybe he'll get some answers
now. Bearce pulls over to wait for the vehicle to pull alongside him.
It seems to be taking its time—almost, he judges, from reticence.
Maybe he had surprised whoever it was. They hadn't expected his
tail-lights after rounding that curve. Hell, he is taking his time!

Moving slowly up behind him, James Fay is doing a nervous
tattoo on the steering wheel of his BMW, trying to make up his mind
whether or not to proceed. He has turned off the late-night Christian
broadcast, considering: *There's no turnout here, but I could back up
till I come to one:* He thought he had seen an overgrown track
probably leading to an old log yard a couple hundred feet back down
the road. ...Don't think I've been up here before. Probably it

deadends at one of those old connected farmhouses ... but I doubt this guy, whoever he is, is going home to it.

This associate (—Fay does not like the way the term is being degraded—) this associate of Julius Golding, ski magnate, is also on the track of a mysterious road he thought he saw earlier gleaming on the side of Jasper Mountain in the moonlight. On the face of it, his reasons for doing so varied from those of Lyman Bearce; but if one were to scratch those various surfaces, he or she might find much the same thing. At last he decides to close with the other vehicle, discovering that its driver is none other than Lyman Bearce, selectman and foe of many projects of James Fay, developer. Projects that do not necessarily coincide with benefit to Bearce's own.

Soon there are two sets of lights aiming up the dark road, a road in fact long used by the descendants of a single proprietary settler of Lot 32 on Jasper Mountain. The recent deluge has not defaced its long-settled and compacted surface, but the many decades have dwindled the parcel of the original inhabitants' descendants to almost nothing.

The Twerp, thought the old lumber baron as a pale car cruised to a cool stop beside him, its window gently lowering with a hum.

"Mr. Bearce," acknowledged James Fay with a nod—as this Massachusetts transplant's sister Gloria had taught him to do with these truculent old Mainers. Fay's head for business does respect the man enough to notify his social soul to be on best behavior. The other looks him in the eye and nods slightly, a reverse nod, barely discernible. His arm on the open window frame, Lyman Bearce waits for the bespeckled young man in the plush driver's seat of the other car to continue the conversation—if there is to be one. It is dark here below the trees, but the great white beard of Lyman Bearce glows faintly on his chest. James Fay represses his cool impatience and tries to focus on that beard. *Facial hair.*

The two men sit in their respective little caves, sending pounds of carbon and other toxins into the air for every half cupful of fuel they expend: each hoping the other will give some reasonable sign however slight for his presence. The lumberman could sit there like a glacier, appearing immovable while slowly grinding away the earth beneath him, for a millennium. In contrast, the dynamo salesman of Jasper Mountain ski resort feels the length of each half second as though it were glacier upon his soul; and so he speaks. "Nice night." It was an uncharacteristically brief conversational gambit. He was learning.

Bearce considers this observation with contempt. He would say nothing to the Masshole ... but for that thing that is on his own mind. Instead he says, "It was." It was not going to be to any advantage to treat James Fay the way he would as a matter of course. He thought he had learned all he needed to know to deal with James Fay.

"One good thing," said Fay, smoothly choosing to ignore what might be construed as an insult, "Ceylon Segar's business dealings won't do any harm to your trees—with them being such big carbon absorbers." It was maybe meant to insinuate camaraderie in superior management technique.

The response was typically hasteless. "If it don't turn dry enough fah the fire to creep through th'roots and turn 'em back into carbon."

Fay felt the relief of his new advantage: Bearce was making conversation. It was a refreshing moment ...of an almost friendly leisure. It was not a middle of the night's seeking after...? There was a new road, certainly, ahead somewhere; the possibility of a new way opening, and perhaps here was the man who was making it happen. There had been talk of the Bearces' beginning to consider opening up some of their land to the purpose ... the only purpose, really, for Jimmy Fay to even be in Gottheim. (He sometimes thought this now that things were not going so smoothly with Theodora; of course the tire fire was eventually going to go the way of all flesh. Then development would pick up again.)

"There's that." He said nothing more. He was getting the hang of it. Soon he would be as taciturn as any Bearce or Kimball or Sessions or Howe.

But still Bearce said nothing. He had only to wait. What he wanted to know was bound to come out soon if he did. The Twerp would never be able to out intimidate someone whose ancestors were not from away. (Because of the extent of Bearces' holdings and his father's longevity in the business, Lyman had forgotten that his own forebears did not help settle this area.)

There was silence, each man looking at the other.

Facial hair, thought James Fay. "Yes," he said, "Just thought I'd come up and take a look at the new road."

It was not quite enough to let Lyman Bearce know what, if anything, was on his mind. Or that Fay was peeved at himself for stumbling into the open....

Or *possibly* into the open...? No, maybe there was no harm in what he had just said. He stared straight ahead into what had become the wet dust of the headlamps and tried to think of the beard. Then he said, "It's reached us."

The light of their beams was bouncing back into their eyes now, Bearce saw. He was not going to find that goddamn road tonight. Not with this ash fall. Not unless Fay led him to it. With that almost imperceptible reverse nod, he rolled up his window. But he did not leave. James Fay activated the passenger window, and he also sat there. What do you do now? He drummed his fingers on the wheel, wondering what Bearce was up to with this parcel. And who was its owner if not him? He turned the radio back on.

~~~~~~~~~~~~~~~

Eloise is caught out in it again. If she had a nickel for every time she'd been caught in a snowstorm, freezing rain, sleet or lightning-and-thunder ! Wouldn't you know it: Ceylon Segar's tire fire has caught up with her on unfamiliar ground! If she were at least on an unfamiliar *road*, a lane, a cut or three-wheeler trail—but the willy-wacks! How were they supposed to get out of the woods?

She felt for the small polished horns and ears of Sheila, comforting herself in the feel of soft hair covering the bony head of her goat.

They were fumbling through thickets and under the high rustling boughs of pine through a dense black mist, a drizzle. It was no use trying to sit it out somewhere: There *was* no where. No, it would be better at least to keep fumbling downhill. Not like West Virginia, with its roads on the ridges of mountains. Here if you fumbled downhill long enough and then resisted the urge to go up another hill you were bound to run onto a track, or at the very least a stream ... which would have to empty into something. That was one good thing about being in the mountains. Down East in the flatland—in the real Willy-Wacks—you could go all night in nothing but circles and come—again—nowhere.

Hmm ... let me see ... where was I? Oh yes. The inhabitants of Goatham were all rabidly discussing the misfortunes of those exalted members of the exalted order who had been inexplicably and surreptitiously poisoned by ground rhubarb placed in a coffee urn at the Grange Hall.

She tried to block out the illustration in her mind: There was the counter at D'catter's Diner with its black baldheaded proprietor sitting on his stool eating Yorkshire pudding and beyond him, visible through the order window, his Eurasian niece flipping tostados. [Show outsized tostadas with falling toppings.] Standing behind the counter gossiping her head off was Alabama

Persimmons, her huge dangling circular earrings flopping back and forth with every yak.

"Just like Decatur's, isn't it, Sheila?" Eloise tried to crack herself up.

It was no use. Her formerly white jacket was now black and nearly soaked through, her hair straggling into her eyes, her glasses hopelessly blackened and fogged. She kept taking them off to wipe on the insides of her overalls pocket, but it was no use. She tried to make herself *walk straight* —through the brushing understory, over the blowdown, over boulders and feeling for ledges. But it was no use. She tried to make believe that they were not coming to any ledges to freefall off, any ravines to tumble into, any stone walls to...! A stone wall! Yes! She tried to make herself believe that she was going to find a stone wall and follow it out along some old settler's property line into the open. But it was no use. Then she felt for Sheila's head again. The lanolin comforting her fingertips: This was useful.

"See, what it needs is a tavern of some sort—like Farmingham Royal Inn—to be called ... Fatham! Yeah! *Fatham Inn and Tenpin.* And the landlord keeps pet rats in the basement to entertain the customers.

... Because ...he doesn't really *want* any customers. He's not like these new small business owners that have come in trying to make the place quaint: He is like the locals—doesn't really want any customers—can't stand to see 'em coming—is cold, stony, just stares at 'em—and his wife—his wife is Irish and she is sick of not having customers and she's drinking up the bar and she wants to go back to Ireland!

But it was no use.

She was shivering now. If she were going uphill she would want to trend toward higher ground on the finger bones of the hill— avoiding the innards, the small ravines. But now a small ravine would be good to creep into, follow along down to—somewhere. She had been here long enough to learn something of how to get along in the woods. Not like when she first came and got herself lost, got herself scared, got herself turned around in the woods. And that was when the sun was shining! Of course now, all these years later, you've got weather, you've got a tire fire, you've got a black night. You've got shivering, you've got.... She sniffs, sniffs again. You've got bear. ...Smells like bear.

"Now don't go getting scared, Sheila. It could just be rotting vegetation. You know that happens this time of year—you get that smell, almost as big as pig—bear smell. Sometimes even bigger. Maybe it's stinkbugs."

The goat seemed uneasy now. Eloise went down on her knees and stroked and stroked the bony head. She sat back on her haunches and began telling herself a joke in her loudest deepest voice. She did this for a while and the smell did not disappear and the wet rock she was sitting on got colder, wetter, and harder and Eloise decided it was time to get up and move on again despite the horror filling her nostrils. "Sheila," She said at the top of her voice, "That is the largest most frightening smell I have ever smelled!" But the heavy black drizzle closed these words in on her. Shivering, Eloise and the goat moved on.

Down and down they went, and they brushed through some saplings and seedlings, and there was a bare spot and then more seedlings, thickets and trees again. And Eloise thought, There was a bare spot ....

She retraced her steps as best she could and found a hard bare spot again. She got down on her knees and stretched, and felt this way and that, and realized that here was a path. Eloise got up and felt for Sheila and walked along the path, testing to see which way it inclined: gravity would be her guide now.

God is the ultimate hard-to-get player, she thinks, feeling her way over the bones of the path, feeling for the polished horn of her goat.

~~~~~~~~~~~~

Daniel Twitchell is moving through the greasy dark, feeling his way through blowdown and puckerbrush and over the occasional outcropping, trying to make his way up the mountain. Oh man would he welcome that camper just now, the camper he had been beginning to hate—how long ago was that; just one or two, maybe three hours? If only he had stayed at the party until someone else had been ready to leave and willing to give him a lift. Right now he would give anything to have his leather jacket on and be the designated driver of a passel of drunks—puking and peeing themselves and passing out in someone's car.

Or the desert! The desert with no rain. He hasn't been in the Maine woods long enough to know: How was he supposed to find his way in this stuff?

Shivering, shivering.

If he keeps on the uphill he won't fall off a ledge, right? Just keep going up: don't be tempted by an easy down slope. No matter what. Thickets, blowdown, just keep going up. Stay on the high dry ground, stay upright. Stop shivering. —No, keep shivering—that's how you keep from getting hypothermia.

But, shivering in shirtsleeves, Daniel knew. He knew that just going up hill was no guarantee of finding the camper. Blackwell Mountain was too big for that. The sides of its slopes were vast and long, its top was nothing but a series of long ridges, mile on mile. And there was no way to keep on a straight line, like he had been able to do down below when he first got off the track. When the moon had been shining, the black tree shadows suggestive, its light shining on the pages, and the book was in his hand, Phantastes.

> *At length, when the course of the moon no longer permitted her beams to touch me, the night was dreary as the day. When I slept, I was somewhat consoled by my dreams; but all the time I dreamed, I knew that I was only dreaming. But one night, at length, the moon, a mere shred of pallor, scattered a few thin ghostly rays upon me; and I think I fell asleep and dreamed. I sat in an autumn night before the vintage, on a hill overlooking my own castle. My heart sprang with joy. Oh, to be a child again, innocent, fearless, without shame or desire!*
> — George MacDonald

⁓⁓⁓⁓⁓⁓⁓⁓

> *The stories she told were those of her travels along the river, of her adventures among the wildlife, of odd backwoods characters from her forays into deep wilderness. She liked also to tell the tales of her hero Culuscap, the mythic Dawnlander who had some characteristics in common with her Lord. Culuscap was the human embodiment of heaven and earth. He was, if not actually born of his grandmother, then raised by her. He had a mischievous or evil brother, was always ready to accept and meet challenges, responsible for creatures, and helpful in forming the surface of the earth. This mythic Dawnlander, while full of a sinewy temperament, was also capable of being temporarily deceived. There was a persistent, lingering belief among the natives that Culuscap*

*would return once more to help restore all things.
The English scoffed at this, asking when his dust
would rebuild itself into skin and muscle and bone;
when would it grow eyes and see again?* —Jasper
Mary

"Daniel! Daniel!"

Chrischana was in the maple thicket on the downslope of
Buck Hill, below that tiny clearing where the evaporator sat covered
until it should be needed again in the sweet sapping season of next
late-winter. She had taken the trail down past it and was now in the
pathless thickets of the black storm, calling out for her son.

She was a normally calm phlegmatic person, silent even in
the throes of violence, the violence of another, rarely of herself. She
knew how to have the inner conversation, but in silence. She could
weep with grief or regret in her closet, her closet which had become
the out-of-doors when she worked there. She knew how to wrestle
with God. Peter Prince, she knew, wrestled with God too, but Peter
Prince would get bent out of shape by it. When Chrischana
Twitchell got sick in looking around on the world she would say
things like, "When I say come, I mean stay, don't leave me." She
wrestles forthrightly with God. "This is Your great creation, Yours,"
she would say. "Don't You sometimes feel just a little bit ashamed
of letting your creatures get into the shape theya in?" But still,
Chrischana Twitchell was not bent out of shape. She had been
pummeled by all kinds of grief and had seen terrible things ongoing,
but still she kept her posture, gave up no ground. She knew what
she believed in, and who.

"Daniel! Daniel!"

The ground she was walking on had been absorbing the soot
and carbons and toxins of millions of American and Canadian tires,
off and on, for the past three months. This little accident had
convinced her for all time that there were no policy-making stewards
concerned enough to love and care for the earth and creation the way
God commanded in the Bible. There were no stewards but her, and
all the little people who were trying to plant things and grow things
and nurture beings, and just—just do their jobs. ...Without
compensation but a living. Why should we ever have anything more
than a living, she wondered before God.

"Daniel! Daniel!"

Don't leave us. It's your creation. When are you going to
come and judge us?

He doesn't know how to get along in the woods yet. He can maybe get along in the desert when it's dry and cold. He knows how to start a fire with shavings. No one can make shavings in this, she thought, trying to wipe her eyes on the inner breast front of her jacket. "*Daniel! Daniel!*" She stopped to listen for an answering cry.

The sky, your sky, is raining down filth on the creatures of Gott'im, making 'em all sick and ruining their habitat, and losing themselves in your storm. The storm that you and the Devil and your creatures collaborated in making. When are you going to come and judge us? Don't you see how much better that is than just letting us go on and on until the blood is up to the stirrups?

Oh please bring back Daniel. Oh please keep Daniel safe. Oh please bring back Peter and Daniel ... and me ... back safe to the camper, Lord. You are the God of all creation and all creatures, and all the-good-and-evil-doing people and all evil doing devils: You are the God. And the great angels and all the planets and suns and constellations and galaxies and molecules and atoms are yours and your making, oh God.

"*Daniel! Daniel!*"

Stopping her movements, she has silence. Only the sound of the drizzling grease hitting the dead pine needles and leaves at her feet, plinking off the needled boughs and bare limbs above her head.

She whispers, "But I'm not your judge, you are mine."

He is a shivering vessel of grime, misty grime, saturated; a vessel of darkness and sharp things in search of his eyes. He had no eyes he supposes, only trembling fingertips, hands and arms held up to protect his theoretically more valuable members. He might need them some day ... if he ever gets out of this. Daniel is fallen timbers, is legs to negotiate them. He is rocks, piles of rocks to wrestle over. Like some other fourteen or fifteen year-old before him, he is lost on a mountain in Maine.

And he could not see his way through the thick darkness. He came through a patch of seedlings and a bare spot; and thickets of seedlings and a thicket of saplings and a forest of trees. He stepped in something big and soft and stooped to his shoes and came up, himself now a pile of bear dung. Daniel was a vessel of thrills and he was the smell of excreted carrion. And Daniel was the well-loved son of three people in Gott'im, and he was lost in the woods.

If only he knew where he was. Then he would have no trouble finding his way out. No, he thought, it would do me no good: you only think you know where you are when you're lost in the woods.

~~~~~~~~~~~~~

Daniel's father is Balder Simon, Vietnam veteran and lover of Gloria Fay. They would have made it back to the truck okay, if, after stashing their gear and smelts in the pickup, he had not been intent on pursuing a moonlight view of the pond from the ledge for Gloria. It would have been the perfection of the evening had the off-pouring of the tire fire not caught up with them. But now they were out in it, her hand in his.

She did not want to, but she was crying, trying not to let go of his hand, wiping futilely at her nose with her free hand when it was not needed to fend off branches and twigs. If they had not been on the steep side of a small mountain she would have sworn they were in an old cedar swamp, full of those hideous spike-like dead limbs that are bound to put out your eye. If she had known that her guide was flashing back on his war experience, reliving the tropical ash laden mist of the jungle, the sound of a mother weeping for her napalmed child, she would have been horrified.

Polystyrene, benzene, gasoline; incendiary bombs. Flaming jellied gasoline, its targets atomized and falling in the mist. He wanted to let loose the hand and break heedlessly through the jungle, stopping his ears, but simultaneously he was aware that it was Gloria's hand he was holding, and that they were feeling their way through the atomized products of chemical warfare brought down on the house of God. "This stuff came up fom the pit," he was telling her. "Now you see, Glory, why we gut to grow our own food.... Everything the devil brings up fom the pit is uncontrollable by mankind. He's just too good at ducking back into his hiding holes to be caught'n held accountable ana moah."

"Ceylon Segar should be held accountable for this mess," she said, sniffling, dragging the sleeve of her jacket across her nose as she tried to keep her footing on the slippery downhill.

"That ol' fart?—what's he gont do, pay damages out o'the sale of his burning tires, his burning prop'ty? No, it be betta to hold the gov'ment responsible. It give him permission to have all them tires trucked in and stored there. —See what I mean about the devil? That's why he's called lord of flies. We ah the government, we ah a democracy. Who is going to take responsibility for it?"

"Well—they will. —You wait and see, disaster relief, clean up, everything. They'll do it." (*Sniff sniff.*)

He took her hand and kissed it, thinking of the weeping mother. He was kissing Gloria's hand, and he felt he was shedding Gloria's tears and kissing the hand of the weeping mother. Washing Jesus' feet with the two women's tears.

They were dark, blind. Trying to get down a steep face of rock safely. Testing each tree for its foothold in the cracks of rock, something to take hold of and let themselves down. Some places there were drifts of pine needles and dead leaves, the leaves of years piled in the crannies. Everywhere were trees acting as though they were actually going to maintain a long life, hold and grow in these rocks; but many were loose, barely holding, and many more were dead and ready to fall down the mountain. At length they came to one giant too large to get their arms around, and Balder felt along its length, thick ridges of bark, hoary and strong. A giant white pine with massive roots, tenacious in the rock. Its great roots reaching out in every direction on the downslope, like the massive tentacles of a giant squid. High overhead its boughs of thin pointed leaves seethed gently in the foul breath of the falling mist.

"Let's rest here on these big legs, Glory, and see if we get ah bearings."

This seemed doubtful to Gloria, but she was too depleted and discouraged to do anything but settle down on one of the great limbs and lean back against Balder. No, they were not yet lovers in the intimate sense of the word. They were not going to have children. ... Maybe some day.... But not now.

In the camper atop Buck Hill below the summit of Blackwell Mountain two boys had awakened in a familial vacuum. It was their sense of this that woke them, not the tinkling of cinders on the roof, not the wash of ash upon the windows, not even the closing of the camper door. But somehow they knew they were alone together in the world. Of course Nathan and Benaiah did not sleep together, rather Nathan slept with Daniel because Daniel had the required quantity of patience, and because he would never let Nathan provoke him (which perhaps amounted to the same thing).

"I don't like it," said Benaiah from the dark of the bunk below.

This was unusual because as a rule Benaiah would not initiate a conversation with his irritant of a little brother.

"I know what you mean."

This response, with its quiet, even intelligent tenor, was also unusual.

Nothing more was said.

This itself was another aberration. And, for Ben, especially disquieting.

"... Aren't you gonna say anything more?" he asked. This was asked very tentatively.

"I ... think I'm scared."

The incessant tinkling of soot, the speaking of trees on the mountain, the parental vacuum in all this loneliness of the great immane bulk of Blackwell ....

"... Maybe we better sleep together," said Ben.

He felt Nathan clambering out of the overhead. "Bring your own blanket, though."

"Right. You might have cooties."

~~~~~~~~~~~~

Asa was standing in the barn looking at the ancient farm wagon with its wide seasoned planking and old ironbound wooden wheels. It was still half full of bales, the overflow stored here from last season. About half the spokes were missing, he saw. There wasn't much light, just what fell in from the now indifferent moon through low windows and that high one up there in the gable over the loft. He could smell last summer coming off the sweet, almost-green bricks of hay he had put up last year. The bays were over in their stalls pulling in some of it right now. It wouldn't be too much longer before they would be done with that and out there cropping grass on the hillside full time again. Get rid of those hay bellies, he thought.

Looking at the old wagon he was thinking of the coach apparition. He kept wanting to place it, sure he had seen it or something like it, somewhere before. History seems to take ahold of a man, me especially, he thought. And don't waunt let go. Now he had a strange and uncharacteristic notion: What if the apparition *chose* us ... because we know local history ... or thought we did, anaway. He just could not piece this one together. Although he would like to see if it rang bells elsewhere, Asa Bartlett was reluctant to tell any of the other buffs about what he and Olive had seen.

Just then the bell on the tower clock down in Gottheim struck the hour and he listened to it bonging. Tomorrow he would have to go down there and wind it. Time again. But now the bonging got him to thinking about the Village of Gottheim and what all was there, his mind traveling like a ghost over the rooftops and down on the village streets, through the backyards and alleyways.

"Lay 'em away! Townsmen!"

And now he was walking on The Knoll, Crazy Knoll, and looking up at the rundown mansion, the old Victorian Gothic, with its tower and light in the higher-most window. The hermit teacher was up there, probably reading musty old books and murmuring inwardly to himself.... If he wasn't lying on the floor. Asa wondered: Can you keep your wits up when you're that old? Israel Kimball had taught him as a boy in the Gottheim Academy. Maybe he ought to take a walk over there to the school and look around. ...But, no. Instead he went over and peered through the window of the carriage house, two stone's-throw away from the mansion proper. Of course all kinds of houses had been put in or around the mansion since it was first installed over a hundred years ago. And the carriage house had been converted to a garage long since. But now there it was, just as he had remembered seeing it when a boy. Through the dusty dark he saw a big long boxy thing with filthy tattered and gaping covering and stuff piled on it. But there were ironbound wheels leaning against the wall at one end of it. In the light of the moon shafting through an upper window he saw their spokes. And Asa had seen what was under that cover, maybe fifty years ago. From the stone floor underneath its chassis.

Jesus, he thought, coming to himself. What am I doing! ...This is like them kids being on drugs or something. He shook his head and walked out of the big barn into the night. Just seeing Olive again would bring him back down to earth.... He hoped.

But it was enough. Asa had remembered seeing what was underneath that cover from the ground up. He had seen the thing's undercarriage, and it was starting to make sense. Something was. But what sense was it making?

~~~~~~~~~~~~~

Meanwhile, up in the tower, Israel Kimball was peering through age-bleared eyes at those dry little meaningful symbols on an aged page of some old fairy romance from a day gone by. He was reading *Undine*, in French, and smiling to himself. He looked up at the black glass of the window, staring the ancient skeletal teacher of classics in the face. He said, in a voice like a rubble of stones rolling slowly and surely down the drive of the mansion to the lane below: "And I like what they're doing today in books with their characters. Like us, not one of them knows much what he's talking about. ... Nobody knows—except maybe a Prophet of God. He asks us for eggs and we give Him serpents. 'Command these stones be made bread,' we say to God."

~~~~~~~~~~~~~~~~

The two men sat in their respective vehicles moments after the dingy downfall began. Bearded Lyman Bearce, in his Chevy Blazer alongside Fay's BMW, was almost ready to conclude that the evening's opportunities were at an end. Trying to find the new road in this stuff would be a chore, and, unless he were willing to turn his personality inside out and invite James Fay over for a talk, they were not going to have a profitable exchange. The filth was coating his windshield and running down in dark trails. He flicked on the wipers, and gazed into the dingy backwash of the two vehicles' lights. What was the twerp listening to on the radio, anaway? Talk radio ... with music.... Was that a hymn?

Idly, almost without seeing, he kept his gaze straight ahead while his mind worked. Then he saw that something was in their dirty beams of light. At first he thought it was a deer though he knew that deer might not step intentionally into light.

The old lumber baron kept his steady gaze on the creature, carefully scrutinizing it in the dingy disturbing light. It was a dog, probably a coy dog. Ears pricked, its head was turned away and its tail hung out stiff, waving slightly. But then the creature turned, and he saw something he had never seen before, something impossible. Bearce continued to stare. A dog, with the face of a man, was moving slowly toward him where he sat invisibly thrilling. Then Lyman Bearce trembled. He started to fumble with the shift lever, but his great trembling hand was like another creature and he could not make it do as he wanted.

In the pale car alongside him, James Fay was seeing the same through a miasmal mist.

No, it cannot be. It cannot be. These words kept playing themselves over in Fay's mind, and in his working throat, but they would not come out his mouth. The creature looked casually toward him as any alert dog in comfortable surroundings might, its tail waving slightly. But that face—so human despite its pricked ears, its visibly canine ears, cupping this way and that as though listening.

And now James Fay was listening, too. For, beneath the radio hymn, he was hearing remote sounds ... of confusion and chaos. Sounds like the subterranean squalor of insects or formless feeding hordes .... He was not consciously parsing their sounds, but James Fay was aware of them, distantly—as an atmosphere or background of the *mutant* coming toward him. God! How can anything be part human, part dog? He may have been appealing to Jesus, whom he had talked to in prayer many times, sometimes in public at church functions. He was good at public speaking and prayer, sometimes it was mentioned in the paper in Gottheim.

The dog-man seemed to disappear as it moved around the front of the Blazer. For a blessed moment, James thought he had imagined it only. But then, in the apparition's absence, the sounds increased. As a cacophonous background of the hymn playing from the speakers, he recognized the noise: It was almost as though—as though he were about to enter upon the floor of the great New York Stock Exchange.

He felt it before he turned and saw the bland face of a man directly adjacent his own out the window. The sound of the floor came up into his face overpowering the hymnal joy that had surrounded him. But he could not see the face with definition, its shade remaining more a fantastic suggestion than a concrete affront. Dimly, thrilling powerfully with fear, he was aware that the Blazer was leaving him, slowly pulling ahead until it had cleared his bumper, now moving rapidly up the dirt road. The vehicle took off, gravel flying, its red lights swiftly disappearing through the bleak drizzle.

James Fay was left alone with the creature, but the creature had disappeared. No, there it was just beyond the hood ornament, its mangy mantle and stiff tail moving through the lights. Its awful head had vanished downward. *Get out now.*

It stopped, intent on something. Suddenly its—some part of it was erect on the right; and over his shoulder James Fay discerned its movement. Then it was down again. And though the paralyzed Fay could not see what it was doing, it occurred to him dimly in the wilderness of his thought that the creature was leaving its sign on his car.

As suddenly as it had shown itself, it was gone.

Dear Lord, I hope it's gone.

His limbs shaking, James Fay moved the car ahead. It stalled. He turned the key and pushed the gas. It stalled again. He turned the key and did not push the gas. It started. He followed up the road, in wake of the red lights that had long disappeared. Until he came to a ditch the town crew had cut to handle runoff. Trembling he backed into it. Trembling he tried to go forward and the car stalled again. Trembling, trembling. James was able to start and move back down the road again.

Out on the highway he did not know how he got there. Could not remember any of it except the man-dog, its darksome man's face next his own. And Lyman Bearce alongside him. Lyman

Bearce pulling away. The roar and turmoil of the stock exchange floor. It seemed to surge again in the beating of his own heart.

Oh Lord Jesus. Why can't I be light like a balloon?

~~~~~~~~~~~

The Fatham Tavern was dim, pointless, and dark. The bottles under the counter and beneath the mirror behind the bar were dim, pointless, and dark. The clientele were dim, pointless, and dark. The proprietor behind the bar was dim, etc.... The intellectual are different than I and you. This is my story. I am Eloise Patadoe, dramatist and illustrator.

The dim pointless proprietor glared at the dim pointless clientele, of which there were two, so they plunked down their money and beat a retreat into the dim night; mounting up, and riding off from the quaintly hospitable Town of Goatham without so much as knocking the dust from their jingling boots. *I was sitting in the corner with my sketch pad, the one that's delivering these well crafted scenes to you now, and I saw the whole thing.* The dim etc. proprietor would be glaring at me, so that I too would beat a hasty retreat, but he can't see me. I'm invisible, except—perhaps—for my bones. He may be seeing my bones, but he's not letting on. He's an old Yankee and nothing scares him. [Turn page; see picture of skeleton dimly sitting with drawing pad at the corner table. Note its engaging toothy smile.]

There are two kerosene lamps, one on either side of the mirror behind the bar. This is the only light except for what comes through the door when it opens. Moonlight can't stray through the two windows because they are so pointless and dark. Enter proprietor's wife, a thin threadbare downtrodden woman with eyes all over the dim pointless bottles. She struggles to prevent a hundred rats (just up from the basement) escaping into the main parlor with her. With thin hapless hands she thrusts the door shut behind (eyes still all over the bottles). [Dim drawing with round white eyeballs plastered all over bottles.]

"Sure and me darling, you're a sight for sore eyes," she says, ostensibly to her husband, but he's a Maine Yankee, he's not fooled, he knows its for the bottles. He glares at her. This is not one of your middle America hot glares. It is a stone cold non change of expression. He's a Mainer, or did I tell you this already? [Blue painted face on blue granite stone, wearing glasses.]

"Where are the girls?" He asks, referring to their two Irish daughters. "We've got guests, treasure seekers, and I don't waunt'em to be a bother."

Now this may seem like a contradiction—what with him scaring off all his customers with his cold demeanor *on purpose*—but it's like I told you, I'm no intellectual, I haven't got that figured out yet. I'll work on it, because he does definitely scare off all the customers, intentionally, as you can tell by the rats. He refuses to keep a cat for the purpose of ridding them out. [Multitudes of rats creeping all over the bar, peeking out from behind the bottles, and nibbling on the eyes.]

Enter customers, strangers from Oklahoma, who come in talking and laughing and jingling their spurs, and walk up to the bar to say *howdy*. Bartender glares, they turn and walk back out the door, jingling, no dust shaking off. They ride away. [Brown and black drawing of dust sticking to their chaps and boots.]

During the distraction, wife has found a nearby bottle and, scraping off the eyes, tipples some into a shot glass. The remainder she pours down her thin gullet.

The proprietor stares at her, stonily. Of course his expression has not changed one iota since the beginning of the story which is why I can get away with using the same color and ink drawing over and over. [See above.]

"Ah, sure'n that treasure of Jasper Mary's." The slattern no longer notices the stare. She looks hungrily at the shot glass. "Now won't that be a happy day when 'tis discovered. Betther days are cohmin', I tell ye."

"There is no treasure," barked the innkeeper, peering at her intently through the gloom. "The Indian is making fun of us. How many times do I have to tell you."

"Did you want to be saying that so loud, then?" She is cunning enough in this return. "Ah, but there is a betther day cohming sure."

At these words, as though on a signal, unearthly sounds begin emanating from.... Well it's hard to tell just where the unearthly sounds are emanating from. *I'm having a difficult time sketching these sounds. My bony fingers are all a-fumble. Are they coming from the dim plank ceiling, under the floorboards, or from the night-dark outside?* That's the problem with wandering in the woods with a goat on a blighted night while simultaneously sitting as a skeleton in an imaginary historic tavern. I can see the eyes all over the bottles, but can't locate the source of the weird sounds. [Jagged creepy pale letters forming eerie ghostly and shrill onomatopoeia, rippling from every angle.]

The wife's eyes roll toward the ceiling. All the eyes on the bottles look up too.

"The tourists is out looking fah the treasure," he snaps. Naturally the tavern keeper does not acknowledge the strange sounds, preferring instead to interpret his wife's gesture as a hint about the guests. Did I tell you he's a Mainer?

Meanwhile, out in the woods the treasure seekers, with the aid of a Massachusetts clairvoyant, are seeking for treasure. Did I mention they're Massachusetts treasure seekers? Aside from little bells and incense, they've got a dousing rod, presumably one that's familiar with.... Well ... all it's got to be is familiar, right? So far they've dug fifty-nine holes in the woods and what they've got to show for it is a bunch of dug wells. [Drawing of woods with tall trees and fifty-nine wishing wells, charcoal and ink.]

~~~~~~~~~~~

"Where are they?"

"How am I supposed to know?"

"What are they doing it for?"

"I don't know. Now shut up."

"Should we turn on the stove?"

"No."

"Why not?"

"Because we could suffocate or blow ourselves up."

"I'm cold."

"Go get all the blankets off the bunks and bring em here."

Silence. The dark fills up with sound, the incessant plinking of soot and ash on the metal of the camper. Then there is the sound of movement as Nathan climbs out in search of blankets. Now he can be heard and felt piling them on the bunk, pulling out corners here and there to tidy, covering up his brother. He climbs back in with Benaiah.

Soon they are warm and sleeping.

~~~~~~~~~~~

Here is one whose body has become a hindrance to the work of finding its own. It picks its way through the thorny, the dark, the cold and damp. The body is buxom with a long braid that keeps getting tangled in the prickly covering of the mountain. Finally the braid is tucked into its own covering, the jacket on her back. It's a mother, struggling through the wet and dark, looking for one who gives her role meaning. She comes from a line of such possessed of the role. She would not be here doing this otherwise. No one has come here except as Fruit of Coupling. The role fulfillment—or nonfulfillment—is where the pain comes from.

This one happens to be the result of coupling two lineages, Yankee (East Anglian) and Abenaki (Native American), both of whom knew this mountain left and right, up and down. The descendants of the grantee proprietors knew it as Blackwell Mountain, the native proprietors as *Three Faces*. Chrischana Twitchell is the result of seed passed along from the original town father of Gottheim and Abenaki natives, seeded in the mysterious loins of Time. One of her Abenaki fathers actually lived, earning his keep for a time, with the family of the grantee proprietor's son. But Chrischana, if she ever knew, has forgotten this. She cares now only for the living seed. She is representative of her ancestors who ate of the mountain and were in their turn consumed by it.

Away off in a Farmington history class they discussed, in less specific and personal terms, this strange inheritance—some of it pieced together from bits of bones, piles of shell fragments, shards and flakes of stone, and musty traveled documents. They will be mulling over the clash of cultures, of enemies who became relatives, became friends; or regard one another warily.

But listen! The words are crying forth, even as the besmirched creation cries forth its burden of failure and sin.

"Oh Culuscap!" *If such insipid tears can charm you, be welcome to them....*

Her weeping stops. Chrischana Twitchell wonders, *What did I just say?*

Yes, she was praying to that mythic hero of the Dawnland Natives. He who formed the body of the mountain.

~~~~~~~~~~~

The spookiest thing in the woods around Gottheim (usually) is Elda Simon. She is silent, shy, ghostlike, and an animal rehabilitator. Her ghostliness is a suggestion of both her slight stature and the way she moves through the forest, looking for creatures to repair. You may happen on her for a passing interlude and notice in parting some movement of her backpack. She's not likely to say much, but she will never be intentionally rude. Jasper Mountain is her more usual territory, of course, because her old crumbling homestead is above Hutchins Pond on a hillside of that vast monolith.

The wind has been freshening favorably, the weather passing to the great town mountain's hinder quarters, and she is out in the moonlight now, searching for any who may be in distress after the recent day in the dark and ashfall. It's thus that she happens upon the dog-man in the woods on a spur of the mountain above her home.

He sits back on his haunches regarding her beneath the boles of a tall leafless thicket, much as any canid might, who was wild and yet unafraid. The difference is that this one has not taken cover. At first sight he shocks her.

After that start she cocks her kerchiefed head and looks at the creature again out of the corner of her eye. His face is white and gleams in the moonlight, yes, a human face ... with dog's body and ears.

Poor creature.
What can be done?

They continue to regard one another, Elda more carefully than the dog-man. In fact, the dog-man is already bored. Rump in the air, he goes down on his fours, rear high to stretch every muscle and tendon including those in his paws. He trots off deeper into the thickets above, its human face turning this way and that.

He is lost to her vision, and she turns away, convinced that she would have been able to do nothing for him. He is a mutant, plain and simple, and there is no helping the dog part of him, which would have been her sole concern.

"I've gut to tell Balda bout this," she muses, peering into the bushes at her feet. It would be a good way to get a conversation going. Better, she thought, than the thing she'd seen at Rhetta Bearce's.

~~~~~~~~~~~

James was more irritable and nervous than was usual for him. Of course ever since the tire fire, he had not been very happy ... what with the Goldings practically abandoning him to the scourge of the market ...until ... just until the air should clear (so to speak). Theodora sighed and watched him pace about the darkened parlor, touching things here and there, an antique knickknack, a picture frame (ostensibly to straighten it), the half-full glass of buttermilk upon the doily on a small round mahogany table at her elbow. He did not pick it up to finish it off.

She had not helped matters by giving her family's heirloom chair factory to the employees. ...That had been very hard. She sighed again. She just did not know how to help him. Theodora prayed, but it didn't seem to do any good. ...Except ... it helped *her*. Yes, it helped her to pray for him.

It was something she wanted to suggest he try, but that would've been absurd, of course. Of course James was already praying. Of course. Hadn't he been the one to bring her back to church, to point her in the right direction, to tell her about God?

...But it didn't seem to do him any good. Then she felt ashamed—or was it guilty?—for even thinking this.

It was dark here in the parlor, the only light happening in through the hall from the kitchen where there was a night light. She was wearing her nightie and dressing gown, having been startled awake by his ringing of her bell in the middle of the night. He had something urgent to tell her, she decided upon seeing him there in the porch light, his eyes very uneasy through the sheen of his glasses.

"What is it, James?" Her query had been urgent, full of anxious concern as she stepped back allowing him into the entrance hall.

"...Nothing really, Theo." He had brushed past her into the parlor. "I probably shouldn't have come. It's just—I wanted to see you."

He had looked at the mantelpiece clock then and seemed taken aback. "—And, well, we *are* engaged. It'll be all right."

But it wasn't all right. The allusion to what the neighbors might think was not the point. The man she loved, who was everything to her, was distraught. The competent self-assured James Fay was splitting apart at the seams.

"James...."

He seemed not to hear her tentative verbal approaches.

He said, "I don't know why I came."

"You came ... because you're worried. Won't you please tell me what it is, James? You know I love you." Her tone was as soft as dove's down. He seemed not to notice.

"Theo, I don't know why I came to Gott'im."

She stared at him where he stood in the gloaming, just outside the small glow from the small light down the hall. He stood, slight and nervy, a twilight shade of himself, of James Fay, the strong confident mover and shaker, the salesman. The golden boy of the Golding salesforce. He had made her feel she was everything.... Well, at least not nothing. Not like most everyone else made her feel. And now all she could do was sit here like a dunce, saying his name. James. Such a wonderful name. Such a wonderful man. There must be something more. Oh, let there be something more she could do.

"...Well, you're here to live. You came to Gott'im to make a life. ...You thought maybe you would just be a developer, but then you found me." She said this last hopefully. It was her soul hope to encourage him. She hoped he would not remember about the chair factory.

He seemed to consider her words. But then he began pacing again and touching things. His attention had disintegrated once more. He began to tremble.

Her spirit flowed toward him. She stood and put her arms around him softly saying , "James.... Couldn't we pray? ...I know it helps me when I'm scared...." Her voice dropped softly. It was full of calm.

His arms flew up. She stepped back.

"—I'm sorry, Theo." Nervously he backed toward the hall entrance. "Yes, I'll pray—and you pray."

And then he was going out the door and she was standing there in the lamplight of the doorway watching him where he stood beside the dingy BMW, its passenger side. He was just staring at the car. Or—staring through it. He seemed befuddled. A more definite person would have said he *was* befuddled. Theodora did not know such concreteness. But she knew that James Fay was in trouble.

He stared at the grime all over his car. Even now the urine smell of the inverted man-beast pricked his nostrils. He shook his head. There was so much of it. Otherwise it would have washed off in his travels back down into the pondside village. With this and the filth of the tire fire combining, the beautiful symbol of his hope was besmirched. Idiotically besmirched. He felt like an idiot, a crumbling idiot.

Rhetta Bearce watched her husband narrowly, wondering what he was thinking. She could read Lyman Bearce, her spouse of too many years. What he was usually thinking fell neatly into its few categories. ...Something was different. It was a category unknown to her ... unknown to either of them she supposed.

He was walking around in the large glass enclosed veranda. That was the second time he had filled a shot glass in the last two minutes. It was dark, the only light filtering through from the first of two lengthy well-appointed rooms at the other end of the house. And there was moonlight. Seated in her comfortable chair, Rhetta glanced past him out into the landscaped garden she had been working on earlier in the evening. And over there was the crescent drive upon which she had seen the apparition charge her. She was certainly not going to mention it to Bearce. She had had her own shot of gin, with tonic, earlier. That, coming on the heels of her somewhat absurd yet calming conversation with Elda Simon, had soothed the irritation out of her.

"So waya were you, then?" She said it crisply.

He stopped. He smoothed his great faintly gleaming beard with an imperceptibly tremulous hand. Lyman could not shake the feeling that his hands were but two great paws. He downed the Scotch whiskey and his scattered thoughts seem to resolve themselves into these spoken words: "I had to go up and down the washed out road on tother side of Quaker."

"On those knees? Well, I'm sorry to hear it." But it could not have taken him all evening to do that. "So what did you find out?"

"About what?" He was headed to the portable bar along the wall again. But then he seemed to think better of it and changed course abruptly to go stand looking through the glass at the drive. She had the feeling he was not seeing anything visible to her eyes.

Rhetta betrayed no exasperation, as she might have when Bearce was fitting into his known categories of thought and demeanor. What *is* it?

"... About the proposed cut," she suggested after a moment.

Could it have been a dog? Just a dog?

But then that face came back, the awful bland human face in that awful malevolent light. What was he going to do with it? Would it ever go away?

He turned back toward his wife. He tried to look at Rhetta, tried to absorb her inscrutable steadiness. Absorbed, it could last him but three or four, maybe five seconds, he guessed. The unflappableness of his wife was not going to do one thing for him: For that to happen he would have to tell her. He walked to the other side of the veranda pretending to look out on the back garden. ...He could not.... He could *just* bring himself short of it ... but it would never come out. Never. No.

He had driven every village street several times. Fay could see the grime coating everything in the quiet avenues, neighboring houses filthy in the moonlight. Every house, parked car, storefront, the shrubbery, the Common, its gazebo where the Community Band played. The Village of Gottheim, archetypal New England village, a mess. He does not know how he was able to focus enough to recognize, but, rounding the corner again, he saw the Chevy Blazer of Lyman Bearce parked in the street before the Farmingham Royal Tavern and Inn. The discovery startled him. The companion of his distress. The Blazer, Lyman Bearce. Lyman Bearce must be in there.

The age of the man struck him as he approached, through the dim light of this old cellar tavern to the bar where Bearce sat, elbows on the bar. James had never been in the tavern or any bar in the village before. The thick stale tobacco smell almost gagged him. A TV above the bar was on, slanting its light down onto the few patrons' faces. Fay was too distraught to notice anyone but Bearce. The old lumberman was staring into the shot glass in his hand. He did not look powerful. He did not look like Lyman Bearce. He looked old.

But again the dog's human face was intruding upon James's observations. He had to stop this. Somehow. Prayers in the car he had made while driving the village had not seemed like prayers to him. Not real prayers. ...Not even real words. They were flaccid verbal constructions masquerading as meaningful words. James Fay might not have put it like this. He might have said, *My prayers are pointless.*

James Fay sat down beside Lyman Bearce at the L-shaped bar and ordered a glass of Schweppes ginger ale. Hearing him speak, the older man looked up sharply.

"Mr. Bearce," nodded Fay.

The other dropped his gaze back to the glass and grunted.

The ginger ale was set before James and he took a swallow then pushed it back toward the edge of the bar.

"You're going to need something stronger," said the old lumberman.

"I don't. —Drink." Fidgeting, Fay cleared his throat. "You did see it then?"

Bearce said nothing. He finished his shot and ordered a beer.

Suddenly another voice, higher in pitch, intruded itself. "See what? Whad you see?"

They both looked across the bar through the haze of cigarette smoke. There sat the king of used tires, Ceylon Segar. In the ghostly light James Fay looked at him through a decimated expression. He had never seen the singular grubby individual he would have designated "gentleman"—being at a loss for any other term to use on him. But he knew instantly that this grizzled thing was the personage responsible for everything that was wrong with Gottheim.

The small unshaven pinched face that looked as though it were ready to spew a jawful of Kodiak cola was split by a yellow grin, aimed at both men.

The disgust of Lyman Bearce began to reassert itself as he looked at that grin.... There was a comparison to be made between James Fay and Ceylon Segar, he was sure. Both were small and compactly built men: grasping, looking for the deal. Maybe their abilities weren't that dissimilar either, he mused. If you cleaned up Segar (everyone pronounced it Cigar) and gave him a few more brains, a little more class, took off twenty or thirty years, you'd have James Fay from away.

... Except that he knew Ceylon Segar's forebears had been here even before Bearce's own. That the land he owned had been in the family for generations.

Then he remembered the dog-man and its face, and how he had taken off when the creature went behind his Blazer; off up the road, winding, winding until it deadended at the old homestead of one of his own mill hands, Hastings. Hastings, the competent edger with the arthritic hands who had been with them forty years. Bearce had circled in the yard, his beams passing over the dismal dark front of the house and back into the blackened rain. The sight of the house had surprised him. How had he forgotten that Hastings lived up there? It had come into his mind to hop out of the Blazer and knock on the door but just as suddenly he remembered that thing he was usually able to forget or discount. Lyman Bearces' father had cheated some of the Hastings out of a large piece of prime timberland. God, he was going to have to see Hastings again tomorrow in the lumber mill.

It might even have occurred to him to knock on the door, ask for a drink, confess a theft, the theft of his father. But no, there was too much pride for that. Too much pride even to consider the possibility. It was his father's deal.... No sense in bringing it up now. No sense. No sense.

The dog-man with its human face: no sense.

He looked away. Lyman Bearce ordered another whiskey.

~~~~~~~~~~~~

Nathan was whispering into Benaiah's ear. "Dad's coming!" It was not his usual volume of response to the remote thunder of the Harley coming up the mountain road. Usually he was on his feet in a moment, crowing, turning out to greet him. At the sound of the Harley purring through the undergrowth on the lane toward the camper both boys were relieved enough to take up the usual tussle, but now in an uncharacteristic and muted manner.

Nathan tumbled over Benaiah, inadvertently punching his elbow into the other's abdomen before landing in a heap on the floor. Benaiah stayed put, relaxing into his relief, while his brother hopped up and began crashing for joy into things. Two pans that had been stacked on a stove burner fell to the floor with a clatter.

Peter Prince called. "What's going on in there?" Through closed jalousie windows they could hear him pull the cover onto his bike.

"Dad's home!" crowed Nathan. He opened the door and stuck out his head. "It's raining clinkers again!" He had been hearing them on the roof all night, but now he felt their greasy wash on his face. "Dad, get in here out of the clinkers." He thrust the tin door wide. "Nobody's here but Benaiah'n me."

"Nate, this isn't home, it's a holding tank, remember?" He climbed into the dark camper and sat down on the table-made-bed he normally shared with Chrischana. Nathan stood to one side of his knees between him and Ben's bunk. "What happened to your mother?" He circled the boy's skinny hips with his arm.

"We don't know. We don't know where Daniel is, either."

Into the dark he said, "You there, Ben?"

"Yeah."

"She's looking for Daniel." He tousled Nathan's hair. "He's on his way home and it's probably too dark for him to see through the clinkers."

"I thought you went to look for him."

"I did, but I couldn't find him on the motorcycle. You know what it's like when you go into the woods? My bike doesn't go in there, does it?"

Nathan's thought for a moment, then said, "That's bad, that being in the woods in the clickers."

"Now they're clickers," muttered Ben from the darkness of the bunk.

Peter shrugged out of his greasy leather jacket and tried to figure out where to put it. It was a larger version of Daniel's own that he had given the boy two Christmases ago. Didn't he see it on Cindabilla tonight? ... It might keep her from getting hypothermia, he thought. He put his arm around Nathan again and thought of the dog-man. *Wherever you are, buddy*, he thought, *it's home*. Then he began to think of leaving these two and going out into the woods to look for the others.

"Maybe I better go look for 'em."

Neither boy spoke but they were thinking *don't*. Nathan said, "Maybe. What can you tell us, first?"

"God, you don't mean a story—*now*—do you?"

Ben liked it but he said nothing. This was one of those times when he hoped much from Nathan and his nattering, as Dad called it. Often he just had to wait and soon Nathan would speak his own feeling. It was a secret thing he seldom if ever acknowledged to himself.

"Yes yes," said Nathan.

"Did I tell you the one about the man with the dog's face before?"

"I don't think so. Do you, Benaiah?" Nathan turned toward the hole where his brother was lying, silent and still. "Do we want to hear that one—?"

"C'mon, now. I'm here. There's nothing to be scared of. I won't tell you a story to scare you. You boys are good and I don't want you scared, so don't be."

Nathan was jigging on his feet. "Yeah, but Dad—. Didn't you say you weren't gonna be here in a minute?"

"...Trust me. You know in Europe they are afraid of them and call them werewolves. But this one isn't a wolf or a wolf face. He looks just like a man but he's got the face of a Pekingese. Remember that dog that lived two trailers over in Phoenix?"

"You mean Mrs. Marquez's little dog that was so funny? His face looked like a brown hand had flattened it."

"Well it was a flat brown face, anyway. Now that dog was smart. Member how smart his eyes looked? If it wanted to bite you, which I don't think he really did, he'd only be able to reach your kneecaps."

"He chased me once. I shouldn't't've teased him."

"Yes, we know," said Benaiah from the bunk.

Peter grabbed Nathan's arm as it flung out toward the source of provocation. He held firm and put it by his son's side.

"This man had a flat smugged-up face like that Pekingese, and no one loved him for it and this made him mad, of course, but *that* made everyone laugh which made him even madder. So you can see, it was a vicious cycle."

"Kinda like a dog chasing his tail," said Nathan.

"Exactly. The harder he ran after that tail, the madder he got. What he needed to do was stop and realize that he was getting mad, and that he didn't wanna be mad anymore. So then he asked God to help him live with the Pekingese face and said, I won't ask you to change my face, but will you at least help me not be mad anymore?"

"And God said yes," said Nathan.

"Of course. But it didn't happen overnight. Sometimes he had to ask for help again, and then one day he didn't need to ask any more.

"Now get in bed and say your prayers, and if you wake up and I'm gone you'll know what I'm doing, okay? Maybe Nathan better sleep on top?"

"He can sleep here if he doesn't bother me," said Benaiah.

"Are you going to bother him?"

"No."

"Okay then."

Peter took out a cigarette and started smoking in the dark. In the dark the boys watched the light of its ash move from his knee to his mouth and back again. Soon they were asleep to the sound of the clinkers.

It sounded to Peter like one of them was wheezing. That was new. He went to check who. It was Nathan.

~~~~~~~~~~

Demon got loose and was prowling through the woods looking for deer to harass and destroy. This worked best when other dogs got loose and joined in. Of course demon was top dog and any other encountered would, after the ritual sizing up, be invited on prowl with a mere glance over the shoulder. He was bristle-haired and black, with long white teeth in a grin accenting his almost slant-looking eyes. With regard to ownership, Demon was a strange combination of Cindabilla's and her Uncle Ferddy.

The latter was a brutal sot who made tolerable his days by making them as intolerable he could for others. It was not too long after Cindabilla accidently shot him in the butt (with his own bird gun) that he purchased this awful hybrid of a doberman and wolf. He had felt the need to arrogate a little top-dogging in the household so that his niece might see what's what. He needed, he thought, more respect from her.

But she was nothing if not contrary to him and soon had Demon eating out of her hand and answering her call before that of Uncle Ferddy—who had never been quite able to divest himself of the fear he felt for the hybrid. Demon had not come to the household as a pup, but as the nuisance castoff of an apartment dweller in Lewiston. It happens that Ferddy can read—a little—

enough to spy something unusual in the classifieds when a notion seizes him.

But Demon was the terror of the neighborhood. He had attacked a girl who had known no better than to tease him when he was tied to the dilapidated shed of the dilapidated farmhouse the Sessions lived in. Naturally when he got loose and saw her again he went and took a bite out of her. Her folks had thought that since it was her own fault there was nothing they could do in the matter. They would not have been inclined to call the police, or animal control officer, to complain of their neighbors' failure to control. Besides, they were drinking buddies.

Here's Demon on the scent of deer on the wooded hillside in the gleaming night above his house. He's alert and excited and already tasting the whole flesh of deer molecules lodged in his brain via direct connection to his snout. Suddenly he's checked by another, stranger, scent; one he has never encountered ... or has he?... It is either a man or a dog. Or —? It is a senseless commingling of smells making the hackles of Demon rise. He keeps trotting straight ahead but now his ears turn this way and that, alert for any clue to the forthcoming encounter.

He sees it stepping through the moonlit trees, the crosshatching of shadows and light on the hillside; its own ears visibly cupping. And that face, the face of a man unperturbed by his presence.

Demon is not prepared. He slows his pace but advances, tail at a slightly uncertain angle, his ears as high as he can get them—not all that high. It is not a time for hostility but caution. The other dog—was it?—also advances but without checking itself first. Its tail is high and its neck arced. All this confidence Demon recognizes for having experienced it in himself. But it is that other part put together with it, much as his own has been put together, hybrid that he is.

If he ever thought about such things he would realize that he is rattled. He would recognize in himself the signs he has witnessed in the other dogs, the underdogs. He is the dog that tried to attack Petey Prince right through the windshield of his pickup in subzero weather, the dog that sent him back to substance abuse counseling the night Alvin Robichaud froze to death in his own truck parked next to Petey's. If he has feared not man nor beast why fear the combination? Is there something more here?

Demon must stop and let the other come. The stranger approaches, swift and stiff.

They are opposed, neck by neck, hackles raised. Ears low, Demon inquires, looking directly into the human face whose eyes are averted. Demon turns slightly away. Tentatively, he lowers his snout to sniff the other's groin and is frustrated by a sideways hop. The other's tail is high and his strange head continuing averted. His interest in Demon appears small.

Suddenly, at no apparent sign of aggression, the stranger knocks Demon's haunch with his own, casting him momently off balance. The wolf-hybrid's tail goes down and he turns to watch his mangy superior tear uphill through the barred moonlight. The human face looks back once over his shoulder and Demon follows, his tail, though a bit higher, still drooping.

Already Demon senses where they are headed for he knows the lying down place of deer; he knows their trails and frequents and slaking pools, much like you know where your neighbors live and work. He has harried deer from these places before. He does not need to be an opportunist. And he does not wonder that the new top dog knows where to go.

Up the side of this mountain and, rounding, down the dogs go. And there they are, not a little way up from a drinking pool, resting and chewing their small cuds. In a moment the deer are all gone off, but one.

The stance of the top dog checks the flight of the undisciplined Demon after them. A sudden, if remote, sound of a thousand growling, coupled with an almost casual glance is enough to stay him. So he looks on the one left behind, the white deer he has glimpsed once or twice before. It may be that this whiteness is an indication of illness. Or it may be a sign of injury. Not yet a yearling, it seems not so wise as the others who have scattered even as they tempted chase.

See it standing there: so brightly reflecting moonlight in the midst of a chill unleafed woodland of mud-season Maine. Its shoulder twitches faintly, but otherwise the deer seems to have reverted to that trancelike protective feint of its early months. The animal rehabilitator, Elda Simon, had once seen such a youngster in a tug-of-war between two coyotes. She knew they were coyotes and not coy-dogs as was commonly supposed in the region. Coyotes had made recent incursions into the state, perhaps from Canada or even New Hampshire. She had seen firsthand what such wildness will do. But she had also seen the pets of her neighbors so destroy deer. They would tear open a fawn and stupidly watch its life sink, agonizing, out through that brokenness.

The white deer will be easy prey. Delicate and fine as enameled porcelain, it stands— not ten feet away as they watch.

But this is *not* the instinctive eyeless trance of innocence. This is a true *look*—complete. And unlike what Demon knows of young deer. Yet there is no actual expression beyond that which says, *I am deer*. Here is the language of a body completely without fear.

Demon glances at the dog-man, who moves to circle with lowered head, it's chin leading as though a snout. Demon licks his chops, gulps, and starts opposite.

The deer leaps up and moves away, the others in surprised pursuit.

Through thickets and stands gleaming with bars of heavenly light the chase carries up and over the slopes of the mountain above Cindabilla's house. On and on the deer leads them, mile upon mile and the dog-man's thousands howling ... over deadfall and down ledge, up the sides of ravines. On and on the sheen of the white deer leads, on and on until they are passing together into the raining atmosphere of ash and black night where its gleaming hide is almost extinguished, and still they pursue like a horde.

Comes a flickering break in the darkness, though dog-man's howling continues as ahead a new rumbling threatens to overcome it —the breaking and bursting and blowing; the roaring of fire pots from melting cast-off tires, its hellish glow firing distantly through the fall of its up-sending fury.

Straight through dense black downpour the white deer leads them, still leaping over and through the grimy wreck of woodland. The dogs' splayed paws tear up the leaf mold in their panting pursuit. Excited Demon feels no bounds. He adds his snarling and snapping to that of invisible hordes, even as the fire mushrooms before them.

At the top of a knoll, scrambling, they see the fiery skirts of the billowing black crust, taste it in their nostrils, follow toward it furiously. Having not once overlooked its shoulder: Down the white deer plunges before the moving volcanic semblance, its white hocks, forearms and hooves working without stop. Leaping the dike installed by firemen to contain both runoff and the conflagration, straight into the fire it goes.

Translucent, aethereal, the white deer stands amid the heat, flames and thunder, only now stopping to look back upon the hounds of hell.

Demon stops in his descent, tumbling end-over-end in his already scorched and frantic withdrawal. With canine flexibility he scrambles to his feet, drooping, quaking; bristling, swerving away.

The dog-man follows the white deer over the ditch and dike into the fire.

Demon has gone back through the blistering heat, the drizzling oil and soot; circling back the way he has come toward Sessions'. Had he stayed to glance back from the hilltop upon the outpouring of hell below, he would have seen two tiny creatures, one in flames.

Igniting in foreground, and from deep within, explosions send jets blazing upward, momently parting the dense moving cloud. Had he stayed to listen Demon would hear multitudes of men screaming, scorched and cursing, their filthy blasphemies rising in toxins, not distantly nor remotely, but pandemoniac loud. The cries are extinguished in a burst of flame and the dog-man is gone. Only the deer remains in the fire and fulmination, testament to God's own spirit of repentance, purity, goodness, and grace.

When the all-volunteer firefighters of the rural towns surrounding Gottheim first arrived on the scene in little Quaker Plantation weeks before, they, with all their trucks and equipment, were together for the first time since the Jasper Mary Day parade last summer. (On that day they came gleaming and screaming along Front Street to the delight of the assembled children, their elders grimacing.) The scene before them on Jasper Mary's legendary treasure ground, now tire dump, was unlike anything they had ever seen either live or on TV. In a rush of adrenaline that would have powered the creation of the earth itself, they set to work with backhoes, hoses and ladders, pumps and lines leading up from surrounding streams and the River Birch. They knew there was nothing they could do to extinguish the hellfire that was spreading before them. This was a stopgap from which they would be lucky to escape with their lives.

Men and equipment came up from Guildford and even Lewiston, and still they were stop-gapping this fire. It was winter and cold, sometimes with subzero weather, and where there were not explosions and conflagration, there was misting ice. Some places both men (and equipment) could scarcely operate, and some places they were in danger of heat prostration.

In company with the state fire marshal's office, the suits from the Department of Environmental Protection came up from Augusta to oversee the work. Initially, when they had seen what

Ceylon Segar was up to, and slapped him with a pile of fines for illegal tire dumping, on second thoughts they reasoned that the tires had to be someplace, and, under their tutelage, decided to license him. They showed him proper pile size, fire lanes, etc., made sure his bucket loader and other equipment were safe and inspected, and before you knew it Ceylon Segar was a proper businessman and quasi pillar of the community, though he still smelled bad. If he did not do everything to the letter—and some of those piles got to be big as mountains, big as a ridge of mountains—he would be more than happy to explain why.

Lightning *will* strike. If anything can go wrong....

Foam retardant, by the tankload, was tried with no result except an increase of toxins to the flaming brew, surrounding aquifers, and streams. That's when they brought in the pump panels, deluge guns and firefighters from as far away as Bangor. Also the EPA, FEMA, DHS, LURC and the Guildford Salvation Army. By the second day, when it was clear weather (in the north), the black smoke from the fire could be seen on the edge of sight from Portland. People donned their snow gear and climbed to the tops of mountains to look out on a distant funnel cloud, pitch black, as though touching down from a massive thunderhead. Booms to absorb yet more runoff contaminants were set around the original moat and dike.

We will not speak much of the devastation to animals handmade by God and breathed alive with His breath. We will not speak much of the destruction to surrounding woodlands woven out of the particles and elements of God's elegant imagination. Or of the pollution of breath which was meant for the health of the children. The rats We know about.

We have spoken to the stewards of all these things. We are tired of speaking and of their ill response.

We saw the heart of the volunteers and others who came to quell the fire of nature's rebounding wrath. We saw the fertile response of those who care, the Caregivers. And we saw the others, the stewards, behind their desks, on their networking fairways, working away in their fast craft. To the first I say, Watch, guard against influences coming and harmful to your community, strengthen what remains though it's already dying. To the last I say, buy repentance of Me if you can. There are no more words We speak to encourage you.

~~~~~~~~~

"And the rats have all left their cozy homes in the tire dump to make their abode in the hamlets and the village of Goatham. God is the ultimate hard-to-get-player," murmurs Eloise stumbling through the damp and dark, its acrid bitter downfall on her lips. "....Absurd for the self to believe it the owner of the human being with which it's associated, the soul to which it attaches, Sheila. They've studied the Self, you know, but don't know beans about where it comes from. They know how it operates, and believing it to be prime mover of humankind, have elevated its status to ultimate *raison d'etre*. I mean, here I am walking in the shivering dark in tire drizzle, with you for company, and I've found this path and will cling to it no matter who or what tries to get me off. Is there anybody else here with us? There's you, me, God, and Self. Remember, you can't get away from God no matter what. We are living walking bones and, make no bones, the rats are also with us in Goatham.

"We need to get back to the Fatham Tavern for shelter or we might not make it home tonight. We've got to save the Irish lady, and all those rats in the basement, because ... because.... Well anyway we just have to. If we keep working along at it enough, it'll show us how those bones got loose in the woods. That's my plan for making it back to the house and the other goats, got it?

"....Those bones had a definite body language, don't you think? What can you tell from it: them being scattered all over the graveyard and that gaping door of the vault.... Like maybe they were in there first and somebody forgot to bury 'em—? Or maybe they were "interred" there and got dug up by critters. —Or maybe they decided to go out and walk around, quite forgetting they had no skins to hold'em together. Maybe they were family and had a brawl in the graveyard."

Her grimy glasses had long since been stowed in a pocket of her overalls. Sheila's bell tinkled faintly beside her. Eloise held onto her horn alternately stroking her silky bony head. She shoved a stringy piece of hair behind her ear. She jammed her hand back into the pocket of her jacket and trudged along the bony spine of the path.

"Do you think we'll ever find that graveyard again?" Do you think they've been dead long, or were they mass-murdered last year? Have you ever noticed that it's hard to talk through chattering teeth? I'd be warmer if I were sitting in that tavern and these teeth were nothing but a grin in a skull instead of a chattering skull grin in a tire fire rain."

She had been stolid and silent then talkative by turns, and now it was time to be stolid and silent again as she willed her legs along the path.

~~~~~~~~~~~~~

Daniel Twitchell cannot stop his teeth chattering nor his limbs shivering, violently shivering, as he stumbles through the woods. His shirt and jeans are plastered to his skin by a fine rain of not forty degrees. Maybe it is time to turn around and try going down the mountain instead. It is all beginning to seem one to him, but he has a recurring idea that he will keep warmer through uphill exertion.

The name of Donn Fendler has long since gone out of his mind. Earlier he felt the ghost of the lost boy walking with him; probably, he then reasoned, because he had read Donn's story. Whatever became of him after that, Daniel had wondered; after he wandered the slopes of Katahdin, lost in the Maine woods, for so many days—or was it weeks? Did you grow up and have a career, get married, have kids? Did you become a policeman or game warden? Did you ever go into the woods again? .... No, you didn't find a book named Phantastes and get scared out of your mind while walking along reading in the moonlight. There was too much else on the mountain slopes to scare you. Things like thinking your knees are hinges. But aren't knees really hinges of some kind? Something to enable you to open and close your leg, lengthen and retract your legs as you walk? Could knees ever rust shut?

But all that careful reasoning is over for Daniel now. He knows himself to be lost beyond recall. Even such fatal certainty fades as heat and health sink out of his lithe body into the night. The requital of nature slowly absorbs the essence of his being upwards into its gritty diffusion. His mind is withdrawn into its own center, softly sleepwalking and inchoate.

Daniel rouses in the falling snow. The blowdown that he climbs over are wet and white with it. It pelts like sleet down his lashes and into his eyes, its formerly bitter taste turning to salt on his tongue. He has climbed into a white clearing and, Look, it's a man and boy! He tries to call out to them across the way where they are sloughing through the snow on snowshoes. They look over at him briefly before turning back on the way with their weapons. The boy has a gun and his father bow and arrows. On their backs are an ash-splint basket for the boy and basswood carrying bag for his father. Daniel does not know how he can tell they are father and son, nor why the polliwog style snowshoes seem familiar. But didn't he see something like that hanging in the shed next to Balder's everyday snowshoes? They are the kind Indians make and use. ...But I am an Indian, thinks Daniel. Why don't they come here and help me?

The boy and his father are gone in the thickly falling snow, dissolving into it as though they had never been. His hope sinks within him and he begins to cry, quiet tears falling, mingling with the smear of his face. He lies down in the wet tangle, folding together shivering as though he would shake apart. "Jesus, Jesus," he whispers through clattering teeth. The teeth in his jaw, clashing together, seem to have outgrown his body, their clashing is like the pitching of great limbs in a storm overhead. Daniel heaves himself up to continue his wandering.

But something is standing there in the drizzly snow not far off; standing beneath the boughs of white pine: sifting in and out of the snowfall. At last he sees that it is a tall Abenaki, robed and mantled in blue with a hood of worked blue and white draping his head and shoulders. In his hand are tall bow and arrows and he stands regarding Daniel through the pouring snow.

"W-w-will you—?" whispers Daniel.

But softly, thoughtfully the Dawnland Native regards him before fading back into the snow.

Now Daniel stands with his back against a rock wall, cold, damp and furred; a rock with barnacle bumps along its surface. It's a ship with wooden hull.

He feels with his hand, trying to pluck plates of lichen from it. A rasping voice startles him and he looks up into the great face of a man with raven-like beak staring down on him.

"You are pulling on my plumage," the voice croaks. "Maybe you better stop now."

"Sorry." This is a sullen mutter from the mouth of a child who has been greatly wronged. "You don't look like a real person, anyway." *I should be taken away from here in an ambulance. They should give me warm cloths and hot chicken soup. At least give me some stinky quilts or a pile of dry leaves to crawl under.* He is silent, indignant and grumpy in these unvoiced thoughts.

"But I *am* a real person. I'm a folk of the forest, with the same body parts as yourself ... but perhaps made out of other materials. For instance, parts of my hands and arms, unlike yours, are delicately hollowly boned—many such delicate bones—my scapulars far stronger than your own. And my long fingers, unlike your own, are feathered. The cartilage of my nose is without skin, and horny, while yours is bulbous and soft. We are like the People who thought of us—arboreal creatures. Did you know you are going to die?

Daniel began to cry again, softly. "Yes, yes. We're all going to die. The Lord made us this way."

There was grave silence. Everything stopped except the snowfall and the heedless tears.

Said the queer man quietly, "Why d'you s'pose he did this?"

"So we wouldn't get swelled heads like the devil. It's prob'ly why he does everything."

The Forest Folk gave what seemed an involuntary gurgle. Daniel was a moment deciding it softly raucous laughter. He had taken a step back when the rock spoke to him, but now looked fascination at its wings. "I'm desperate," he said. "Can I get under there?"

Anyone who knew Daniel would have been surprised at this forwardness.

The Folk opened his wing and Daniel entered into its shelter, surprised by the soft thick dry down of its interior, and pleasurably grateful. He stayed there a while, standing beneath the sheltering wing, shivering, before poking his head out to say "How do you keep it so dry and cozy in here?" He drew his head back in and leaned into the thick down against the man's warm side.

The folk's voice seemed both muffled and as though it came vibrating through the upper part of his body next to Daniel's head. "Of course you know that without my outer feathers the down inside would be saturated and of no insulating value. In fact it would be the worse for me. Maybe in the first draft of me it was such, the same as it is for baby birds, but then seeing so many dinosaurs and birds and forest folk walking around plastered and dying, God probably decided another draft was in order, so he evolved these structures over the down in my arms and hands. You can feel along them with your fingers if you like. Notice the lattice-like structure and how the contour feathers are covered over by flight feathers, which shed water like one of your raincoats. Of course I can't really fly with them—yet. I'm waiting for the resurrection, I suppose. When the Lord will descend from heaven with a shout and I will rise up to meet him in the air."

"Are Indians suppose to be believing that?" Daniel assumed his own voice to be muffled, as he felt the comforting pressure of the other's wing in a momentary hug.

"They don't have to. Nobody has to. But then look at Culuscap. Didn't he help to form, or formed, these mountains and the way they are dressed? And wasn't he sort of attacked by his evil brother, and supposed to be coming again? Of course, I don't know about that up in the air part regarding him —myself.

"This conversation is making too much sense," murmured Daniel.

~~~~~~~~~

"The vocabulary of Mainers' body language is a small one," seethed Eloise through chattering teeth.

"You take those bones up there somewhere in the lost graveyard. Their body language is all over the place, they could be saying any one of a number of things now that they're dead. But when they were alive? Very limited body-language vocabulary. In fact, they only know how to say one thing: 'Go away.' But it's probably a good thing they can say even this much in body language because they're too taciturn to say it with speech. Take our tavern owner over there at the bar. He can be as talky as he needs with everyone that's not from away, but look how he's dealing with those treasure hunters from Massachusetts.

"[Lots of crosshatching, chiaroscuro, more light localized around the bar where stone-glaring innkeep is making tea for the abstemious treasure seekers.]

"In thickly crosshatched shadows the plain little group dressed in typical nineteenth century garb cowers beneath the stony gaze of the barkeep. They of course have long since lost their own native Bostonian suspecting and puritanical outlook on the rest of the world. The garrulous great-hearted high spirited Irish have seen to that. Up here, in their grant-fostered independent and unconscious solidarity, Mainers would not allow the minority Irish or French to make a dent in their so carefully placed rock walls. But I digress.

"They drink their tea in silence at the circular table usually reserved for card-playing loggers and river men when they aren't getting wood down to the mill. (Yes, I am trying to get a little history in here, nevermind that Maine was a dry state during this period long before Prohibition. Some of you will overlook the fact if you want to have a good story. For authenticity's sake we should go down into the cellar, where the rats are, to dip into the cider barrel, but instead we will have our California folks belly up to the bar.)

"[Open door reveals white moonlight illuminating strangers therein. Enter the Californians with big smiles and good hair. Tavern owner stares stonily as they approach talking rapidly and eying his skinny wife who is still trying to scrape her eyeballs off the shot glass in her hand. Big rippling onomatopoeia of scary sounds emanating every which way.]

" 'Fascinating atmosphere you've got here, sir,' flashes one set of big teeth in the direction of the owner. [Talking balloon in the shape of a megaphone.] 'This would make a tremendous setting for one of Mr. Edison's moving picture shows. The West would have nothing on you!'

"Barkeep looks at him.

"Unfazed, the Californian talks on: 'But what we really have in mind for this area is *bingo*, you guessed it! Yes, high stakes bingo, that is—once you get this tire fire business cleaned up, that is. But it's never too early to plan: that is, plan BIG! Naturally we're here to do the talking for the Native Americans. Just between you and me, we know they're not much better at talking with outsiders than you Yankees, right? (*wink wink.*)'

"[Collection of big hair and teeth, with sharp eyes looking around at strange noises emanating from every which way.] 'You really should have that plumbing looked at. Here's my card. Don't worry we'll be in touch.'

"[The teeth, eyes, and hair throw a last glance at the tattered Irish lady and depart back into the moonlight, voices trailing.] …'Did you see that skeleton in the corner taking notes? What do you suppose is holding her bones together like that, what keeps her femurs attached? And what about those bony fingers holding that pen! We have got to tell them about this in Hollywood ....'

" 'Rich-bastids,' says the tavern owner, shoving the card across the bar to his wife. 'You can't trust 'em. Says here theya fom Nevada.'

"She picks up the card and, squinting, pretends to read it in the light of the guttering lamp. 'Aye, hoosband. Sure'n didn't I tell ye betther days were a'cohming?' "

~~~~~~~~~~

Engine running, Balder and Gloria are sitting grateful and warm in the old pickup. The heater is roaring and they are wrapped bare together on the bench seat in an old Indian blanket Balder normally keeps draped over the seat-back. It is black night under the pines and raining soot, their breath steaming the windows. They are happy and snug in their own little Balder and Gloria world.

"Now what was that you were saying to me about that dismal guy last summer? The one said food growing couldn't keep pace with population." Balder stops kissing the top of her dirty wet head long enough to murmur this.

The kisses and murmurings are making Gloria weak in the thighs. She misunderstands what meaning there may be—if any—in the words. She asks a question to stop the weakness from spreading. "—Dismal—who?"

"You know: the reason we caunt make babies." It is still but kisses and murmuring, soft as gently falling surf.

"Malthus," she said. "The dismal theorem. ...Yes. ...He had it all figured out ... mathematically."

"Then it's a math problem ... we caunt make babies."

Gloria chuckles, happily.

"Don't worry, Glory. God's got the problem figured out. ...He's good at math." Balder tightened his hold on the blanket, tightened his arms around Gloria.

"...But if you look at Ethiopia...? ...Look at Africa. ...People are starving. Malthus was right."

"So God doesn't have it figured out ... doesn't know how to care for the people we make." He kisses the greasy shell-like ears on either side of her head.

"Well ... I won't blame it all on him. I mean ... humanity hasn't done such a great job of keeping the planet stress—less ...." The last syllable is said after a sharp intake, on a sigh.

"...I like a sweet woman who thinks." He bends his head gently to her responsive lips.

But it is no patronizing verbal trick, these words. She has just made a profound concession. It is their first time.

~~~~~~~~~~~~

Afterward, they snuggled together speaking softly about this and that. "You've been happy ever since you discovered your son Daniel, haven't you Balder?"

"I was getting happy when I found you, and then he came ... and that made it pretty set." It was yankee understatement, she knew. She would never get it but she wasn't sure she didn't like it.

"The most solemn kid. You should've seen him helping me on the house last summer. I could tell he didn't want to. He's generous, he nevah said a word. Volunteered to help Mutha build her loon nesting islands. Ah, he's a great kid, Glory."

"You think we'll have one of those, you and me?" She did not want to say that she wouldn't know what to do with one, but Gloria could not help thinking it. She sighed again. She would think all about that ... if there ever came a time.

"If weah lucky ...."

What did it matter if they were naked and in love and never imagining the tedium and turmoil, the mysterious deep magic, of long life as one? They drifted off to sleep in the mythic Balder and Gloria world.

~~~~~~~~~~~~~~~

Asa and Olive were lying in bed beneath a big sheet of divided-light moonlight. They too had had their connubial embrace, but now lay back together under warm handmade quilts, wakeful. The bed, with their combined slightly porky weight, was sagging; soon Asa would be leaving for his own room. Easier on the backs of both that way.

He was saying, "I think I figured out where 'twas I saw that thing before." They had seen the great apparition and heard its distant echoing cries together on the Lower Intervale Road earlier, yet Asa was not about to reveal his extraordinary—hallucination— was it?—in the barn. That was just too much sharing for him. Maybe he was coming down with Alzheimer's, and if so it wouldn't do to let Olive know. She'd find out soon enough.

"You were bound to," she said. "I read somewaya that answers come fom the subconscious when you're not looking."

That was some comfort. Not much. They were both staring out at the big bright moon.

"Don't it seem funny. We ah looking at sunlight shining on us fom that," he said.

"Evah thing's weird if you think about it too much," said Olive tersely.

That's why I'm telling you this, he thought. So's I can stop thinking about it.

"So where did you see it?"

"Must've been fifty years ago, but .... In the carriage house of the Gothic mansion on Crazy Knoll waya our old schoolmaster Israel Kimball still lives. Don't know if it's still there, but 'twas under a canvas tarp that I lifted and saw the carved pillars and glass panels, then I crawled underneath and looked up and saw stamped on the bottom: Grable & Sons. When I was a teenager I read up and found out they made hearses, this one being of the mosque deck style. But when I saw it there as a kid it was on top of an automobile chassis. Evidently, early in the century it had been used to that other purpose, but I nevah found out show-a." He turned his head slightly to look at her, noting the marble-like quality of her eyes.

She let her gaze slide from the moon to his face, noticing the same quality in his eyes. Must be something to do with the moonlight. ... Pupils reflecting moonlight reflecting sunlight.... Too much thinking. "Wouldn't it be fun to go visit ah old schoolmaster? Think o'all the stuff he could tell us about the old days."

Asa turned back toward the moon. Gawd, what Israel Kimball wouldn't be able to tell about this place fom the last part of the previous and the early parts of this century, thought Asa. Wicked smot schoolmaster like that. He didn't say much, but back then he knew what was going on as well as what went on in Greece two thousand years ago. Still gazing at the high silver disc, he said "Jeezus, his mind's gone by this time. He won't know a thing. Prob'ly in diapers by now." He said this last ruefully, thinking of how he had ditched his underwear in the middle of the compost heap by the garden before he even got the horses bedded down for the night. He'd be strapped into a wheelchair in no time.

"Well," she said, "what would it hurt to see? Yuht, he's been a hermit all these years. But you nevah know. He might waunt to see us. He was a good teacher, waunt he?"

"Daow, I misdoubt his marbles is scattered all ovah the top floor of his tower."

"...So it's a coffin carrier 'stead of a circus wagon?... Was he—or whatevah it was—saying he wanted to put his cargo in the ground, think maybe? Whad it have to do with us, wondah?"

"Nothing," said Asa. "That's the way ghosts is. They got theya own business to mind. If we just happen to see 'em while doing it...."

"That's not what you said during your talk last summer after collecting all those regional ghost stories, Asa. Sometimes it's got something to do with the one who sees it."

Asa thought then of the story about the young girl at an evening's musical in the last century, seeing that dead infant at the window and crying out 'twas hers, she'd done away with it. ...But the others present said it was her own reflection.

~~~~~~~~~~~~

She could not see a blamed thing. Oddly, she was thinking of the state social worker she had had a conversation with in the grocery, a person the size of a small office, who thought there was something wrong with a neighbor who gave birth to twelve kids. *You have to woo God. God is the one who conceived the personal. It is impossible to approach God in any way but personally. One-on-one.*

She was blesséd. She was alive. She had come down the dark mountain through the tangled greasy wet woodland and out onto the hottop. Eloise wobbled down the center of the blessed road, still feeling her way with her feet, her hand yet reaching down every so often to touch Sheila, her goat. She had no idea what road she was on, it was still dark and drizzly, and she was shivering, but she was alive. Alive. It was a real road, and going to take her home.

She was thinking doggedly. *I don't care if we get hit by a car, Sheila, I am not budging from the center of this road. Dying by automobile is better than hypothermia. At least then they would have to take us to the hospital. I would shoot them with their own hypodermics if they did not take you with me.*

Already the lurid glow of hell surrounded her, its whining demons coming for pathetic Eloise Patadoe. She was not even going to make it to Gott'im or Quaker or wherever this road was taking her. They were squealing and screeching and swerving onto the gravel behind her, heavy fat things. Who would have thought that demons could be so big. She kept walking.

A car door opened. "You! What are you doing in the road?"

She recognized the dry glooming voice of the bellyache's editor. Eloise turned back, facing into the grizzled misty headlights angling for her. *You are in hell, too, Mr. Nutting?* She wanted to ask, through chattering teeth, but could not make herself. She had to get home, she turned back again.

The hands caught up with her and turned her around. She stood her ground; faced into the gaunt sidelit sallow features and nut-like eyes of the editor, scarcely recognizing him without his green visor. "D-d-don't you feel naked?" she asked him.

"Ms. Patadoe," he said. "You and your goat had better get in." Hand and arm were held out toward the light firmly, an ushering gesture. He saw her disheveled features in the greasy light, the lank strands of hair, the tips of her ears peeking out. He saw she was obstinate, numb.

The touch of his grip was surprisingly gentle if firm. Eloise allowed herself to be guided to the car. She watched as Nutting opened the rear door and suggested she put Sheila in back. "In the backseat of your car?" she asked. "I don't think she'll go in there."

"She will if we make her."

"Yes, that's right."

She was never able to remember afterward just how they did it, but soon she was strapped into the front seat of Mr. Nutting's car, with Sheila's dark head between them. "It smells just like wet goat in your car. She ought to be at home in here."

"Yes," said the editor dryly.

The head withdrew itself, the bell tinkling wildly, as small hooves behind them began thumping and clattering restively.

"Take hold of her collar or whatever you've got for her," he commanded.

"You don't have to get huffy," said Eloise, huffing.

They rode several miles with the heater blasting, Eloise alternately aimlessly speaking or silent, shivering. Nutting was on his way back from a long day in Augusta, where editors of Maine local weeklies annually convened, and now he was glad of the distraction to help him keep awake on the road. At last they pulled up in the yard of Eloise's dark house on the Quarry Dog Road.

"You know w-where I live!"

"I know where practically everyone in and around Gott'im lives." He reached a hand across and opened the door, got out and swung wide the back door for Sheila. He came around and helped Eloise to her shaky feet. "Where's your keys?"

She dug in her pockets and came up with her smeared glasses. She put them on, took them off, dug around some more and came up with the keys. He gently pried them from her slow bewildered hands, quickly took the steps in the filthy diffused light of his highbeams, and inserted the key. Eloise followed, smelly, hangdog. Tinkling faintly, Sheila followed them both. Nutting flicked on the light by the door and Eloise stood in it, blinking, amazed.

There it was, just as she had left it, the kitchen still full of unsold paintings in crates, but otherwise neat except for a few utensils and crumbs on the counter where she had made the snack she brought with her on what was to have been a short hike. Jim Nutting was already in the next room. She heard the squeal of the woodstove door, the scrape of a match coming from the next room. She walked like a sleepwalker toward the sound.

"Good you had the fire laid. Maybe you want to get out of those wet things—a hot bath." Numbly, she unzipped her jacket and he helped her peel it away. He went to hang it on the peg by the front door and turned to see her fumbling with the buckles on her overalls. "Maybe you better do that in the next room, or upstairs— maybe the bedroom where you keep your dry clothes." He does not, after all, know where most everyone's bedrooms are.

Eloise went up the stairs between the two rooms and before long he thought he heard water running. He checked the stove to make certain the fire was going — the draft was good but not perfect — and went back to the kitchen to peer into the cupboards and come out with a can of soup. When Eloise came back down in pajamas and robe the front room and kitchen were warm, there was soup bubbling on the stove, a pot full of steeping fragrant herb tea, and what looked like buttered bread; yes, it was buttered bread—bread from the freezer she had made before going to New York. Soon it was all on a tray, and he was bringing it into the parlor in his purple-stained hands. She backed into the rocker he had pushed toward the stove and sank down into it, gratefully. The light in the room was that of the stove, what came through from the kitchen, and a small dark-shaded table lamp behind her. He set the tray on the arms of the rocker and said, "Don't rock."

Eloise was no longer shivering but her normal ebullience was flattened. Because he didn't care for it much in anyone from away, Jim Nutting was some grateful for this, but on second thoughts, he thought it a bad sign. Eloise ate, staring into the fire. At last she looked around, saying, "I thought Sheila was in here."

"She's eating. I took the goat out to the—barn." Eloise had another old house outside that had been moved there from down the road specifically to serve as both barn and roost for her goats and guinea fowl.

Eloise was silent. She munched the stale bread. She took a swallow of tea. "They all get fed?" No old Mainer could have been more terse. She was not from away now. She had lived here five generations and was beat down by it.

"Yuht. You okay now?"

She looked up at him standing there to one side of the stove near the kitchen doorway. Eloise noticed that his head did not look as bald as it usually did when he was wearing the green visor. He had sandy hair and a now invisible bald spot. "I guess that means you'll be going. Want to take some goat milk cheese with you?"

"I don't like goat milk cheese."

"So you've told me." He had never been willing to barter ads for cheese. She took another swallow of tea and thanked him for bringing her home and for taking care of Sheila, making the fire and the food. "You don't seem like a Mr. Nutting anymore," she said. She studied him lounging against the doorframe, hands in his pockets, regarding her levelly through his glasses.... *You've added to your body language. It doesn't say, Go away.*

"Jim, call me Jim."

"...I discovered a discrepancy in the townline between Quaker and Gott'im." She was handing him a scoop. As an afterthought she added, "I found a bunch of loose bones in an old graveyard. Humans."

~~~~~~~~~~

Damn tire fire, thought the editor of *The Village Voter* as he drove
back through the falling filth toward Gottheim. He was now
thinking of the nut-case goatherd artist from away.

~~~~~~~~~~~~~

The chrome lines of Decatur's Diner gleamed in the moonlight, its
front also dimly lit by the one streetlight at this end of the road
before the loop to the highway. Early morning dark. Unusually, one
of the fluorescent lights inside was also lit, dully flickering. Baldheaded Jeffy Decatur sat at the counter on the edge of darkness. In
the haphazard light next to the opening where the waitresses could
stop at the kitchen window to pick up an order. The place had been
closed since 3:00 p.m. yesterday, and he was talking away as though
to himself but in reality to his niece Gildy who was in the kitchen
doing prep work. Gildy Hart was getting a jump on it because she
was not going to be there to see to things today. Decatur was going
to substitute in his old place at the grill. Thinking to spare him the
early rising, she came in to ready tuna salad, chowder, gelatin, and
puddings, but he had insisted on keeping her company. Suddenly
the glass door opened and he turned, shocked to see Rhetta Bearce
enter.

"Turned out to be a nice evening after all," she said, seating
herself on the stool next to him. She gave him a moment to get over
it before turning to say, "Don't you think, Mr. Decatur?"

"Who's that out theya with you, Uncle Jeffrey?"

"It's just me, Gilda. Rhetta Bearce," she called. "I saw your
light on and thought I'd step in for a bit of conversation. I'm not
after coffee or anything."

Gildy Hart, a net covering her auburn ponytail, looked
dumbfounded through the order window beside the coffee urn. She
did not think she had ever seen Mrs. Bearce except in the broad light
of day when the older woman might be enroute to some volunteer
organization or club meeting; more rarely grocery shopping or going
into the post office. Never in the middle of the night.

"That was a nasty batch of it we had, earlier; I was just
mentioning to Mr. Decatur." The older woman was dressed in a
tweed jacket and felt hat with speckled feather cocked at a stylish
angle. Her hands were clasped in front of her on the counter, a small
gold wristwatch peeking out from the velour cuff.

"Yuht." It was all the young woman could think to say. To
compound the surprise, she was recalling all the old gossip about
how much Mrs. Bearce secretly hated the diner where her husband
frequently conducted business, in his apparent scorn of the suite in

the fine old office block on Front Street. Yes, she was quite sure she had never seen the dignified matronly figure in here before, though Lyman Bearce owned the old dining car and lot it sat on. She looked at her uncle, as though for help.

But Decatur was never any sort of help in such surprises, and was always the worse for it. His pasty Anglo-French face stared drop-jawed at his landlord's wife a full five seconds. Then he remembered to shut his mouth and look away.

"But maybe you'd like a nice cup of tea, or instant coffee—?" Gildy was able to get this much out. "—Yuht, guess we got dirty again." Her glance slid furtively to the big round fluorescent clock on the wall.

Mrs. Bearce hesitated. Gildy did not think she had ever seen her do this, either. "... A cup of tea would be nice—if water is already on the boil and it's not too much trouble."

"Got it right heah," the other said, her head disappearing from the window.

Rhetta Bearce slid from the stool and moved past Decatur around the counter to the order window, saying, "No need to bring it out, Gilda."

As Rhetta brought cup and saucer back to her place, Decatur thought he heard the faint rattle of ceramic and looked to see a slight trembling of her hand. She sat, removed the tea bag after a moment, blew on the surface and took a sip, then turned to smile benignly at him.

"It's been awhile since I seen you in here," he said. From anyone else it might have been a sly or leading statement, but from this gentle puddinghead it was an innocent recognition of things as they are. Yet, he was trying to figure it up and he reckoned never. —No he misdoubted he saw her in here when she was a teenager several years his junior. His father had had the place then, and Lyman Bearce's father was the landlord.

"That so?" It was a typical response from anybody hereabouts, little more than a tacit ascent. But it could lead one to go on. Decatur realized he had nowhere else to go with it.

Rhetta Bearce was thinking, *But I was in this place last summer.* When it was sitting in our backyard behind the garden. She had had some sort of victory then. Not victory over Lyman Bearce, exactly; over herself. Yet she was not thinking of this any longer but of her husband's Blazer parked in front of the tavern. More, about how troubled he'd been earlier. Probably still was. She had never seen him troubled like that before. For some odd reason this was comforting ... to sit here drinking this tea. This was where

Jeffy usually sat now, she knew, next to Lyman when he was at the counter with the mail, sitting where Jeffrey is now. It was the only way she could think to act out solidarity with Lyman.

~~~~~~~~~~~~~~~

Theodora Prescott heard the car come to a stop in front of the house, and looked up. It was silvery dark in the bedroom, the moon's light and streetlight fallen in predictable pattern, adding drama and even mystery to the room's pretty tasteful furnishings. She rose from her knees beside the bed and went to peer out the front window. There was the roof of James's BMW gleaming dully up at her. She waited for its door to open, but it didn't.

She stood there some moments, looking down, waiting. Then she sat on the cushioned window seat, gaze fickering off across the Common toward the shadowing gazebo, and then back at the car roof.

Down in the car he sat with his arm on the rest, gazing off down the street, seeing not parked cars and empty sidewalks but *the dog.* The dog that was a man, or the man that was a dog, or whatever it was—that awful thing he had seen while looking for possible development properties. He was still seeing it. His time in the tavern with Mr. Bearce and Ceylon Segar had not helped beyond showing him that he was not going crazy. It had shown him too that he was not going to join some cozy fraternity with Lyman Bearce. He had failed to grasp—they three being each be of the brotherhood of businessmen, it could not make them anything but enemies, for such is the ultimate nature of a fraternity based solely on its profession. Though he had seen the same creature, the lumber baron was not going to acknowledge a mutual—anything. As far as James Fay was concerned, Ceylon Segar belonged to the same misbegotten race as the dog.

.... But man was supposed to be God's crowning creation....

The ungodly are not so, but are like the chaff which the wind drives away. Without are sorcerers and dogs.

"But you're my savior: 'Its leaf also shall not wither; and whatsoever he doeth shall prosper.' "

Silence.

He raised a tremulous hand and looked at it.

Again he tried to pray. His mind formed words but they tasted of dust and ash.

For the Lord knows the way of the righteous; but the way of the ungodly shall perish.

He thought he glimpsed something ... however slight: Yes, the *way* shall perish. ... Don't let me be on it. He whispered, "Don't let me be on that way." *Please. I do need You. I do. I am that sinner, I know I am. I keep shouldering You ... aside.*

He thought, if I have to see the dog-man, at least don't let me be *with* the dog-man.

Please. He was shivering all over. He clutched at the door handle and pulled it, climbed out. There was the Common, mottled with shadow and light. He crossed the street and walked into the Common, wandering, restive. I can't possibly be .... I am not like Ceylon Segar.

The Pharisee stood and prayed thus with himself, God, I thank thee that I am not as other men are.... I give tithes of all that I possess.

Wretched on the Common, he circled the somber silence of the mostly early spring leafless giants, a few tall red pines with shapely needled limbs. He had to take off his glasses and stow them in the inner breast pocket of his blazer, for salt tears kept running down his cheeks as he wondered for the first time that he might not be saved after all. The roar of the stock exchange floor rang relentlessly in his mind, that awful bland dog-man face was stuck in front of his own.

"Let me just stand near You, then. No matter what. I know you came for sinners. "You won't stand off from me like that Pharisee."

He was standing in the shade of a Norway pine, murmuring. If he had been asked, he would've said it was an evergreen. He leaned against it, wiping his face, heedless of getting resin on his coat; its smell like Christmas in his nostrils. He felt some relief. He lounged against the pine, much as Jim Nutting had lounged against the doorpost, between the kitchen and front room of the artist, wooing her. "I know you won't desert me, though I am a sinner. I know you won't. I know you won't."

It was not as the psychologists say, "Methinks thou dost protest too much." A true lover cannot protest too much. Not when his or her attention is undivided.

~~~~~~~~~~~

And there was Peter Prince walking down the mountain road in the ugly falling ash and mists. He too had seen the dog-man, he too was seeing the dog-man. He thought maybe he had seen the dog-man every day of his life. Even though James Fay had only seen it once to recognize it, there were comparisons to be made between the two men. Although one grew up in the Midwest and the other in New England, both were children and entered adolescence in the same evangelical denomination. Both had mothers who were and still are pillars in their respective churches, their fathers only nominally so. They are of the same generation, the Vietnam generation (Fay being five years younger than Prince), and know something of the cultural pressures of revolt and subsequent assimilation into the established order. Both men are likable, willing to extend friendliness. There, seemingly, the similarities end. Fay has a graduate degree in business administration, and is proficient in sales technique and interpersonal communication, when working. Peter Prince is prone to violence and he is a college dropout with technical training, a skilled blue-collar worker. He works in the paper mill. He knows he is in trouble nearly every day of his life, and so tries to live them one at a time. He does lean on the Christ, much as James Fay is doing at this moment under the pine tree on the Common. Unlike James Fay, he knows himself enough to know that, for all this true sweet leaning, his nature remains unchanged. It is not yet time to be changed.

Peter Prince was smoking one cigarette after the other as, occasionally stumbling—especially on the upper track—he felt his way down mountain in the dark and falling mist, calling as he went. The tiny glow of his cigarette was comforting to him and he thought it might help anyone close enough to see, but it gave him no satisfaction to smoke for it was too dark to see the toxins parting from his bronchia and lungs on the exhale. Once he got below the highest leg before their camp, the going was easier for the road was packed and crowned and comparatively wide. His calling was interspersed with coughing, hacking, and spitting. The dog-man was still visible and sounding in his soul and he remembered to pray, if feebly. Peter Prince was discouraged, his heart was low because of his sins. He'd been the cause of the abortive search, the turmoil of the night, and the loss of Daniel. Why would God want to bother with him?

But it's them. It's Daniel and Chrischana, and I know they are good enough to bother with. You're good enough to bother with, good enough to trust.

He thought he heard a tiny distant voice in response to his own, calling. He stopped. Yes. It was too remote to tell, but he thought maybe it was Chrischana's voice. He called again. Cigarette still between his fingers, he cupped his hands around his mouth and gave several shouts. He stood still, listening. The voice was on the left, far off in the woods. That would mean she had crossed over the road at some point, for the direction was not below camp but more towards Gottheim. There were still several miles between the village and their part of Blackwell Mountain.

For many minutes Peter stood; smoking, calling, listening, as gradually the sound of her voice grew distinct and he knew she would find him in the road. Now he was hearing her movements in the brush, twigs snapping and cracking. He called again and puffed harder on his smoke. She would be standing beside him out of the thickets in a minute or two.

He waited to hear her speak and, as she stepped out into the road and brushed herself off, he came near and held up the cigarette to look into her face. It was dirty and solemn and, as ever, he could not tell if she had been crying.

"You didn't find him." Her syllables were hard, clipped, tense. "I didn't either. What ah we going to do? Do you know what time it is? I don't know how long we've been at this, d'you?"

The first thing Peter thought of was his training under Herman Gottesman. "Chrischana, I left you in a foul mood and disregarded some good advice from you." He did not say he was sorry, for those were words he had spoken often in the past, falsely, though at the moment of utterance he believed them true. Instead he made a mere confession.

"I know." She was not interested in confessions now.

He suppressed a self righteous urge and suggested the thing he had been thinking of all the way down the hill. "We need help with this. More people searching."

"But it takes so long. One of us will have to go back up to get the truck and go make the call. Balder will come right off, and know others to get. We could call the police, rescue workers, the Maine Warden Service, evah body."

"What about that nearest farm down there on the Lower Intervale Road?"

"Betta. You keep walking up and down this road calling. I'll go down to Roebuck's and make the call." She started off and was gone in the darkness before he could speak.

Remotely hearing its hundreds howling, he resisted the urge to go after, grab her and make his own suggestions, hand out the orders. He was afraid, but not in the same way as James Fay. Both men were in the throes of seduction: For James Fay the uncovering of his own purposes in their true nature was frightening to him. But Prince was drawn by the dog-man's naked corruption, seduced with a strange hunger to consume himself and others in his own anger— leap from its sides straight into the pit.

Walking back up the mountain in the dark he thought about Balder in the war. Balder had to have encountered the dog-man in Vietnam. He could not have escaped doing so, Prince reasoned. He wondered how Balder did it. There was a lot of shit under there, had to be. Sometimes he thought he could see it. Highly controlled shit, but you never got a whiff of it. How could the man be so damn good? He was a walking grin-machine. Petey was sometimes glad to sense Daniel's annoyance over that grin. *He* didn't have a predisposition to addiction; he wouldn't allow it.

Time to be ashamed of myself, he thought. I am ashamed. He flicked the still-glowing butt away. What did you make us for?

~~~~~~~~~~~

Blessed are all they that put their trust in him.

James stood outside the glowing pool of light cast by one of the decorative streetlamps that had been placed around the Common by the benevolence of the ski magnate Goldings. He had been walking in shame, but now stood looking out across the street toward Theo's house with its spacious bow windows and the otherwise straight clean lines of its front. He thought he detected a faint glow coming through from the back where the kitchen light was still on. Faintly, he remembered her conversation from earlier. It had been all but consumed by the apparition that was no apparition ... except in its continuance in his thoughts. Slowly her quiet conversation surfaced with more strength in his mind.

How brief it had been, how kind, tender even. She was so often tender and kind. He thought of this now, displacing his recent irritation over what he had considered her foolishness and weakness. She was without harm, he thought. This usually meant he thought her harmless, but briefly now he recognized the difference in tone between the words harmless and without harm. For the first time it occurred to him that being without harm was a great strength and probably difficult to achieve. Even so, he did not think it would be honest to tell himself that this was an achievement on Theo's part. ...But he had to be careful now: This shame. He was just too dismissive of her. Hers was a gentle soul. And she had been right.

He looked up toward her bedroom window, and there she was. He saw what seemed the whiteness of face and shoulders, bodice. She must be in the window seat. He thought he should let her know he was all right. He should not let his unshakable shame deter him in this. A living presence, it weighted him like a depression. He stepped into the light and held up his face. He waved. The figure moved. Its gesture an answering.

A kind of call and response; not entirely unlike that between Peter Prince and Chrischana Twitchell in the woods and on the road of the mountain, dark with shame.

~~~~~~~~~~~~~

Lyman Bearce was on his way home from the tavern, his senses not yet extinguished by the quantities of Scotch whiskey he had consumed. He was smart enough to leave the Blazer behind and do the legwork necessary to stave off the stupor he was going to fall into. Coming up out of the night shadows of great trees on Front Street he spied his wife's Buick in the lot at Decatur's and stopped dead. He wiped an arm across his eyes and saw it there still. He stood a little straighter, smoothing his great beard with his hand, a woodsman's hand still.

He did not leave the shadows but stood gazing out toward the highway loop, then back at the lot, and the old dining car of the Atlantic and St. Lawrence railway. Drifting down came the distant sound of an eighteen-wheeler floating on its engine breaks, riding large on the night.

What are you doing, he wondered, his thought directed toward the tiny figure of his wife, seated next to that of Decatur in the yellowish fluorescent light on the edge of darkness in the old dining car. It must be Decatur, and he has my stool. Of course.

He stood there, stolid, his hands shoved in his pockets. It was hard to get Lyman Bearce drunk, and he was not there yet. He could still think, steely as ever, but he was chastened tonight (for reasons already mentioned). Lyman Bearce in chastened form is not like you or I. In appearance of manner or action he remains unchanged. As Rhetta has discovered, it *is* possible for something to be working away in him other than pet projects, town politics, business and what's going on in the woods.

He thought, This is the oddest damn night I *evah* had.

He recollected it with due diligence: coming down the washed out road below the lots on these damn bad knees. *Seeing that road I nevah seen before—nor since (ain't that odd), seeing the twerp'n....* In spite of the alcohol, he trembled. And now her sitting in Decatur's, waya she nevah sits—in the middle of the night!

What time is it? He looked hard at his watch. Hell.

Then he stopped and thought again.

It had been years since he thought of it, the cheating of the Hastings.

It had nothing to do with me.

He stood there thinking.

Lyman Bearce started walking again. By the time he got to the parking lot he knew just how it was going to be. Nothing would ever be said. Nothing would ever be known. There was nothing to acknowledge in any other way but what he was going to do.

It was the old man.

He went and sat in the front seat, passenger side, of the Buick.

~~~~~~~~~~

He was sitting at the battered, golden-yellow oak desk going over his notes beneath the glare of a naked light bulb. Of course he had on his green visor. The behemoth press, the old Miehle, stood silent in the center of the room like some heavy ancient iron monster waiting to be charmed awake. Then it would thrash the floor and shake the whole building in its monstrous agony to get out the word. The printed word. Jim Nutting rolled back on his squawking chair and thrust his legs up on the desk. The notes were neat on his clipboard and yellow pad, as complete as he could make them for now. Tomorrow late he would send Libby back to the artist's house in Quaker to get the whole story again.

He reached up a moment to turn off the light, then settled back into the complaining chair, his feet again on the desk. Light from the street fell with its strange orange-pinky glow through the windows. His eyes adjusted to the gloom around him, as he stared out into the almost empty street. Oddly, there was Lyman Bearce stolidly striding with his hands in his pockets, his great white beard spread across his equally great chest above the now-stout middle. He hadn't always looked like that. Nutting remembered when he was handsome, clean shaven, lean—if just as impassively sure of himself.

What a crazy tale. He had been thinking right up until this minute that it was a figment, a product of Eloise Patadoe's ordeal. Even the town line thing he could hardly bring himself to believe. She was from away, after all. What was she going to know about it? ...But then ... he had believed her about the lightning starting the tire fire. How long has she been here? He knew for certain she was here when he came back from Toronto to take over his father and grandfather's enterprise, the village newspaper. It was probably the Nearings ... inspiring her to come here. What a crazy quilt of a place, too, that farmstead.

Everyone who's ever been down the Quarry Dog Road recognized the individuality of: in summer sunflowers and snapdragons and hollyhocks everywhere in clumps; fencing woven out of wire and blowdown from the woods; the house painted worse than a coat-of-many-colors out of perhaps a dozen shades. Someone said it was paint left over from the dump. She ought to fit right in, but she doesn't. She'll never fit in. Hopeless. He smiled faintly.

He thought of her sitting there, deflated, in the front room, spooky front room. A whole shelf full of dolls' heads. One full of glazed pots, several with oversize colorful books. An old Victrola. A large loom with something in progress, probably made out of goat's hair. He looked back over his shoulder and thought the loom reminded him a bit of the Miehle, but wooden. Did it smell like goat's hair in there? It was probably his shirt: He was still smelling goat.

Scattered with bones, an old cemetery. Leg bones. Finger bones.... She did not bring any bones back with her. Claims she had one but lost it. Doesn't know where the graveyard is but thinks she can find it again. He started thinking about the town line once more, stood up, stretched and yawned, and went over to the old wooden file cabinet, which was a match to the desk. ... Well, he might have to go upstairs to the morgue, though.

On second thought he wove his way through the crowded, darkened printshop to the back door, and stepped out into the night. What was left of it. There was the pond with its wide peculiar light. He got into the car beside the building. He would be driving like a drunk if he didn't take care.

The phone at his house several blocks away had stopped ringing. It was ringing now in the office. Jim Nutting drives away. The call received would have been one of desperation. But the editor, old as he was, would have been no use to Chrischana after the night he had put in.

~~~~~~~~~~~~~

"It was right heah," said Rhetta pulling up on the drive in front of the mansion. The moon still shone broad on the steep stately white length with its verandas at either end and porte-chochere side entrance. "And I was right theya." She gestured toward the ragged, ghostly, mud-season garden opposite the curve of the drive.

Beside her Lyman Bearce grunted. "So what'd Elda Simon say about it?"

She responded tartly. "I *did* say she saw the same thing, exactly .... Although she was a little vague about it. But we both had the b-Jeezus scared out of us. Theya's no doubt."

He grunted again, and climbed out of the car.

The drizzle has stopped but the particulate falls in waves, fitfully. Peter Prince is still on the mountain road in the dark, smoking. He's on his last cigarette and thinks maybe it's time to head back up to camp. He's calling, he's calling. There is no answering. On his way up the mountain he is calling yet, but he is also having a recollected conversation with Hermann Gottesman.

"You want to keep it, the very best you have, the whole wad? Throw it away," Hermann was saying.

"But what if it's like pearls before swine? You know, they turn and trample them under their feet. Hooves."

"No, that's what happens when we think the swine are noblemen. We want the attention of the noblemen, so we give them our very best and that's what they do with it. Because underneath... maybe they're actually pigs."

"Let me get this straight: You're saying give the best away to the worst?"

"To the ones we love. We know they are not the worst. But give to them too. Sometimes the worst is just what appears a blind alley. Someday it'll open out into ... what? That's what the Messiah is all about. You believe in the Messiah, don't you, Prince?"

"Do you really think they're different messiahs, Hermann?"

"What am I a prophet?"

And now Peter Prince is hearing an answering to his calls, and there are some moments of call and response, before he realizes that Benaiah is running down toward him in the dark and falling soot. And then it sounds like he has fallen, and he is crying harder and now he is running again. And his voice grows in volume and in sorrow, desperation.

"Dad! Nathan's choking! He can't breathe!!"

Seems the crying he has been hearing is some eerie distant wailing of a siren, for now, having rounded a bend down on the Lower Intervale Road, its sound drifts upward.

He held his crying son a moment, trying to calm him, and heard the siren's wail drift away. There was a strange glowing, coming from somewhere back down the mountain, yet Ben would not be quieted, but kept tugging upon Peter with the insistent desperation of someone not big who would be heard, trying to drag him by frantic force, back up the mountain. Peter encouraged his perseverance, but kept looking back toward the strange source of light, pulsing dirty orange light, he now saw through the stems. As they took the last corner he saw the pulse and glow of light refracting through the falling waves of ash before them, and in a moment a pickup truck with flasher pulled to a roaring stop behind them.

He went over to the driver's side, Benaiah standing by, hopping, anxious and inarticulate. The driver had rolled down his window, letting the ashen air drift in. Peter did not know him in the light of the dash.

It was Moses Merrill, who worked in the Bearces' sawlog mill on the trimmer where, with thoughtful skill, he was able to get the worth for Bearces out of every board. He had been on the way home from his shift when he heard a call on the CB, and being a volunteer fireman, decided to respond. It wasn't that far along the road from where he was at the time. It would be a better thing to do, he thought, than to go home and start pounding back the beers. ... Which was just about the only thing left for him to do now that Lydia and the kids were living with someone else. Knocking around the woods was always fun, and at least he might see if he could save someone else's kid.

"You the one that called in?—Twitchell?"

"Prince. Peter Prince. Daniel Twitchell's my son. But I think something's wrong with the littlest kid—up at camp."

"He's choking!" It was a quivering wail.

"Get in."

They rattled and bounced over the ruts and rocks, threatening to shake the truck and themselves apart as they climbed. After what seemed a lifetime to Ben, they pulled through the bushes, their beams lighting the small taut form lying not far from the truck camper in the now abating fall of ash.

"That's an asthma attack," said Moses, kneeling beside him. "My wife's gut this. Gut get to the hospital!" He was putting the gasping boy into his father's arms.

"I thought I heard an ambulance down below before you got here," said Prince to Merrill as they rattled to the base of the mountain. Moses had reached into the glove box, as they started down the mountain, coming out with an inhaler for Nathan, trying to instruct Peter in its use as they went. Attempts to get the struggling boy to use it were ineffectual. Now they sped at a high rate along the river valley route, the yellow light flashing across the trees and fields as they passed. It flashed reassurance to Peter, on their way south to Guildford.

But back in the bed of the truck Benaiah was holding on tightly to the ring where Moses sometimes secured his dog's chain. The wind blew by him, tossing wildly his hair as he turned this way and that, trying to discover what was going on through the dark glass of the rear window, trying to breathe on his own account, letting the wind flap away his tears.

~~~~~~~~~~~~~

Meanwhile, up in the tower of his Gothic mansion, old Israel Kimball spied suddenly the view out his window. Looking up from his book, he had expected to see his own reflection cast on the black night of the pane, but he found himself looking in the eyes of his great uncle, the one who always wore the bowler.

"Lay them away," said Uncle Hezekiah, his long friendly face—how young!—looking at him matter-of-factly. "It was me, but.... No it wasn't you. T'was me, but anaway....

~~~~~~~~~~~~~

From the fragments of his physical dissolution Daniel thought, But I'm a kid ... I shouldn't have to. *It's cold, so cold....*

~~~~~~~~~~~~~

.... He was warm, as though for the first time. Real warmth, as had only ever suggested itself on earth ... and in grateful Gottheim. The Bright Man of Creation was talking to him and showing him His wounds.

He looked into the fierce glowing eyes, the Locus of all warmth and light, the extreme melting of love.

What happened to the Forest Folk who helped me? Daniel asked.

He said, *I'm He. I made them.*

~~~~~~~~~~~~~

Chrischana was toiling back up the mountain in the thick dark woods. Above, through many stems, spread the ghostly flat suggestion of light to come. "You did the right thing, bringing us back to Gott'im, Mother," said Daniel climbing over deadfall with her. "It was the best thing that could happen to Ben. The best for all of us."

"I know that," she said. "Thank you, Daniel."

She felt him turn and walk back down the mountain.

~~~~~~~~~~~~~

The flat ghostly light reflected as from pewter off the still surface of the otherwise dim river behind him. He turned back. He might have gone through the wall but he stood flush with it, his head one with the small divided panes of the window, his frame stretched out flush with that of the weather beaten side of the tumbledown shed. He was grinning like Balder on the sleeping form of Cindabilla. All the dark solemnity Daniel had ever felt in what we call life was still in him, but now it was as bright as an iridescent blimp.

"Told ya you shouldn't drink like that, Cinda."

For a while (or was it an eternity?), protectively he looked down on Cindabilla, skinny in his leather jacket, her ginger ponytail spread out and lightly frizzing. Then, without turning, he recognized the Bright Man of Creation on the other side of the dark river and, still gazing on Cindabilla, went backward toward Him across the flow again. He turned then toward the glowing eyes of the Man's bright face and said, "Okay." He was melting in gratitude, awe and love, for the Man and His wounds.

They were gone together before they even got there.

~~~~~~~~~~~

"*Ma Mere!*" said Robbie Robichaud under his breath, coffee from his steaming cup burning his fingers without notice.

He was idling at the landing in the cab of his pulp truck, waiting for Ansell, his son, to come up on the skidder. He had just loaded every log that was in the yard from yesterday, but still there was room for more.

The landing was deep in the woods but that did not stop the apparition of Israel Kimball's great uncle with his elegant state-of-the-art mahogany and glass paneled hearse, led by a matched set of great Belgians, pulling soundlessly through the stems on the old track that had once been a county road, a main artery leading directly to the county seat. Gaping, he saw it through the windshield charging soundlessly past. He heard the bowler man's admonition, as though all the way from France on what was here but a suggestion of light from the noonday sun of Reims.

He set the cup on the dash and sucked on his fingers, muttering, "What does he mean, 'Put 'em away'?"

Back down the track a quarter mile into the woods, Ansell had just turned off the rumbling skidder and hopped down to have a few words with Balder. In what had been a vacuum of pale, slow, eerily brightening silence, they conversed, Ansell answering all Balder's questions in the negative.

Ansell's cousin Hiram had set the chainsaw on the clean pale stump he had just made, and the two loggers stood there, the smoke of their cigarettes mingling with the remnants of diesel and small engine fumes; quietly talking with Daniel's father. Then they watched him walk back up the track down which he had come from

a remoter reach of the mountain. Watching him disappear—
slowly—slumping, his towhead faintly gleaming, Ansell recollected
into himself the grief of his twin brother's passing several weeks
before. Froze to death in his pickup outside Sessions' house. He
pulled out a grubby notebook and stubble pencil and wrote
something, fast, to set on the seat of the skidder for his father.

C'mon," he said to Hiram. Silent, flicking their still glowing
smokes away, they followed up the track after Balder.

Such light as this made hardly any difference to Elda Simon, for
whom twilight was not transition. Her days and nights were
something like twilight now. She was in the woods on Jasper
Mountain looking, not for her grandson Daniel, but for Sugarloaf the
deer, son of Posey. White. An albino deer. The sides of the
mountain were steep. She made her arthritic way over deadfall and
carefully past the piercing limbs of the standing dead trees, soon to
be deadfall like the rest.

"Waunt he something good, though, Sugarloaf? ...Why
don't choo find him, like you did that other boy, bring him home?
In't it only right?"

Daniel, Daniel. You just got heah. It don't make sense—
you go now. He just stotted getting to know you. Don't leave.
What would he do, without you?—still carrying Vietnam n'all. ...
back spaceWe was gont set those loon islands we made together in
the ponds. It was going to be what we would do, just you and me.

She leaned her head deep into the side of the white deer,
quietly, gratefully absorbing his musky scent, letting the tears soak
his hide.

Sugarloaf would come at times. He was a whitetail deer.
But he was wild. Untamable. Not like his brown mother Posey who
used to come into the house, eat pancakes, and sometimes slept on
Elda's bed.

The atmospheric cursing of the tire fire had moved off the slopes of
Jasper Mountain and the Lower Intervale and Blackwell Mountain.
And, somewhere, not far from that point high above the river on
which Lyman Bearce had stood to survey in the moonlit night,
finding....

Liquidation Leo stood on the soot and ash and mud of the
Bearce lots road spying out that corner of Jasper Mountain where he
could swear he had never seen a road before. But there it was. And

yet ... was it quite there? In the twilight of this morning, the morning that had not yet fully come. Thank God he had brought his four-wheel-drive beater and had time to check it out before his first appointment.

~~~~~~~~~~~

Below and a few miles to the west, Cindabilla was waking up in the tumbledown shed beneath the orange glow of the divided lights window where Daniel had stood gazing down on her. She looked up at them, thinking, Your arms were out, stood like a cross, I dreamed you was *there*.

She lay still, not quite chilled but not warm either, thinking about her dream. And the bright man. ...Yes. She had gone over the dark river after Daniel and stood there with them, seeing how well He loved him. And she was glad because the dog-man was not. No dog-man. Not if there was ... Him.

She jumped up brushing off the twigs and straw from her hair, from her jeans and jacket, and pushed open the rickety door.

Daniel, she thought, *You're not gont believe this! None of it.*

Cindabilla hurtled across the field that would be full of small corn in neat green rows in another two months.

But as she reached the Lower Intervale Road, she also thought, Betta not go up theya s'early. Chrischana won't like it. So Cindabilla went the other direction, flapping along the road in her shot sneakers. People would be on their way to work so she might catch a ride back to the chaotic Sessions' household—maybe still asleep.

~~~~~~~~~~~

What is happening to me, thought Eloise, that I should be thinking of going to charm school?

It was twilight, and, after her ordeal of the previous night and a fairly sound rest today, she was sitting before the fire gazing on the flames and drinking an apple flavored herb tea. She was tired of playing hard-to-get with reality.

Now she looked at her fingers, listening to the regular ticking of the clock in the stillness of her creatively cluttered living room. She was feeling the finger bones she had held last night, hefting them again, like long loose marbles in her hand.

She heard an engine, the crunching of tires on sand and gravel in the yard. She did not get up. Eloise wished that it was Jim Nutting coming back to hear the story again. But she knew it was only Libby.

She heard the doorknob rattle in the kitchen, where the useless still-crated paintings leaned against the sideboard and table. She heard his voice call out.

~~~ Interlude ~~~

And that was one night in the woods and on the mountains and in the village of Gottheim, Maine. And I suppose there will be a coda after this, and that I may or may not write it. It may be that your ultimate purpose is to save the wayward and evil angels through the wounded shattered fragments of your creation. I don't know. It's a mystery to me how you, making everything and yet being incorruptible, have seen corruption into your realm. How is that possible? But it's here, isn't it? The tire fire, murder and mayhem.

And then there's that well opening on the abyss in that tavern cellar in Guildford. How did bottomless destruction come? Out of God? But you are not corruption. There may be something other than me, but how can there be something other than you?

So now I'll have to write James Nutting, my former student, and tell him about the ghostly appearance of Great Uncle, who neglected his job in the winter of ... well, I will have to research it; and left those bodies in the vault that were supposed to be buried after the thaw. Still up there in that vault after all these decades. And who were they, I wonder? Now let me recollect.... That would make a story all on its own, those folks. Better save that.

That old reflection of mine in the window pane. It's fading as the dawn comes round, glowing orange in the light of that smoldering mess out there. It comes around, the dawn. What was it George MacDonald said, in that book Daniel found and was reading?—

> *My spirits rose as I went deeper; into the forest; but I could not regain my former elasticity of mind. I found cheerfulness to be like life itself—not to be created by any argument. Afterwards I learned, that the best way to manage some kinds of painfill thoughts, is to dare them to do their worst; to let them lie and gnaw at your heart till they are tired; and you find you still have a residue of life they cannot kill.*—Chapter VIII

Yes, and James Fay.... And Chrischana, too. Sometimes we just have to go on and find out who and where our enemies are. Who and what our friends. ...I know. *I'm sorry too.*

This is the story I've pieced out from *The Village Voter*; from imagination, hauntings, gossip, rumor, speculation, innuendo, related to me through my niece from a chorus that is our townsfolk. And I offer it in this notebook from my recluse's cell. Who will it go to when I'm gone, I wonder? I think I've left different notes here and there about where my papers should be going, but I would like for James Nutting to have this notebook. I'm not sure why.

I have not told the story as well as a Jasper Mary could, but I've done my best. I admit it's somewhat disjointed, but cannot help hoping that the reader of it finds some quality of unity in it. And yes, I was influenced by Undine, and by Phantastes in my telling of it. The brevity of this life is one of its salient features. As Moses said: a vapor, coming and going like the breeze, we know not whither nor how.

Oh yes, and, more obviously, Whittier's sampler: The Supernaturalism of New England.

Asa, the kids did not start that tire fire. It was, as Eloise said, lightning. ...Hmm ... it seems to me you're out-of-body experience and subsequent discovery lets me, somewhat, off the hook. Good. I did not really want to write any letter to James Nutting.

I, Israel Kimball, have told the story of how Gottheim came to the point where they might lay their dead away. Now may the Lord do the same for me. I have been in Gott'im all I want and then some. And what's on the other side of Jasper Mountain, I wonder? Shouldn't it be time I got out of this room?

~~~ Afterward ~~~

The sun was coming up east of the maroon and silver diner with Decatur's name in neon. Its interior was crowded before the start of the solemn parade. The coffee redolent atmosphere was humming with clink and clatter of plates and cups and flatware, the buzzing about Hastings' anonymous windfall.

"It's a reg'la mystery," said Robbie Robichaud who looked over at Asa from his place two stools up from Decatur. He turned back and mopped up some congealed eggyolk with a junk of Texas toast. He took a swallow of coffee.

Asa Bartlett was seated in the elbow of the counter, facing out as usual, Olive at his side. "Maybe .... " This small word from the town's amateur historian, was laden with suggestion, prompting Robbie to look sharply back at him.

"You know something we don't?"

"May be," said Olive on the end stool, her large back to the rest of the diner. She was seriously buttering her cinnamon roll. She looked up smiling at Melvinia, who was topping off Olive's coffee cup.

"Prob'ly," said Melvinia Sessions, she with the short gray teased hair, dangly earrings and glasses. "Wouldn't believe the stuff he knows. He once sat down and took three hours to tell me exactly how I was related to myself." She stepped around Olive on her round of neighborly visits to the booths with coffee pot.

"His silence must mean he's gont *keep* it a mystery," speculated Robbie around a mouthful of ham.

From his stool beside Decatur with, on his opposite side, the counter interrupted to allow passage into the kitchen, Lyman Bearce took in the conversation as usual, and said nothing.

"Mystery's abounding heah, of late," said Melvinia, pot in hand, standing by the booth next the door. "They going to get that ghost-sighting, one with horses and the driver with a bowler hat, cleared up? Scared bout ten years' growth off me, night I saw it ovah off Littlehale Lane while taking out the trash."

"That the same ten years you took off for the census in '80?" asked Asa. "Or is this a second ten?"

"Wondah what he'll do with all that money?—maybe quit the edger at Bearces?" Robbie raised his voice on purpose to make sure Lyman Bearce caught this. Yes, Robbie had a job, of sorts, as logging contractor for the Bearces, but that was not going to stop him speaking his mind, ever. He didn't get paid enough for that.

"Daow, doubt it," said Asa. "S'lot of money, but you nevah know what'll happen. He could come down with Alzheimer's or some other catastrophic movie-of-the-week thing. He ought to put it in land. Buy a nice tree farm." Asa smiled—a catastrophic occurrence. Robbie did a double take when he saw it.

"Well, aren't you going to say anything about the old hearse-ghost, Asa?" said Melvinia coming up behind the counter to wash out the pot and fill it again from the urn. The bell by the window rang and she picked up the order for Hiram and Ansell that Gildy had set down. Melvinia waited to see if she'd get an answer before trotting down to the other end of the diner with the tray but Asa had turned back and was murmuring something to Olive.

When she came back, he said, "You can read it in this week's *Voter*. Or you can just attend the service this morning on the

Common. Not only will we be honoring our veterans, but, if you 'memba that story a few weeks back, bout the lost old cemetery up on Morrill Mountain.... We'll be honoring those dead, too."

She gave him an exasperated look. "Where we thought 'twas murder? —Why don't choo just tell me. I admire your great smart history pieces'n all, but I don't have time."

"Mass murder, you thought 'twas, if I 'memba right. All the time it was those blankety kids, of whatever generation, which we'll never know for sure. They always have to find someplace to party'n frig with something—even the bones of theya ancestors!"

"Speaking of which, one of my li'l cousins (save workin' that relationship out fah another time) been telling everybody how she saw a half dog half man. Or was it half man half dog?" and (Melvinia did a double-take in seeing Lyman Bearce actually turn from his pile of office papers to look at her as she spoke.) "Says it happened when they was partying down at the Old Ferry Landing. ...Believe it was the night that young Twitchell died, Balder and Chrischana's boy. Sad."

"Well what can you expect—her mom was tripping out on acid night she was born." Asa remarked as usual on the subject of Cindabilla.

Beside him Olive said nothing, just sipped on her coffee and gazed past the neighboring booth out the window. She was thinking about her younger friend Chrischana, worrying over her like a mother.

"Cindabilla claims she saw Daniel after he died," said Melvinia.

"Like I said." This was dryly put.

"N' you always claiming historical evidence of ghosts. *You'd* nevah see anathin not made out of something."

"Mind putting some intelligence into that thought? And I did acknowledge seeing that hearse and horse apparition. It needed somebody seeing it that had some sort of knowledge about Gott'im."

This time Olive turned to give him a little attentive (and was it amused?) scrutiny. "And just how did you come by that knowledge?"

He ignored her. He had not been tripping out, no.

Robbie spoke. "Said in *The Voter* he saw the identical of the hearse in the schoolmaster's carriage house."

"You couldn't've said," replied Olive cryptically.

"Well, he finally keeled ovah and died. Left a lot of papers too, I hear. Not much else." He grinned at Asa, showing crooked yellow teeth and a renewed ability to razz his friend. He was coming back, just a bit, in the wake of Alvin's death.

"That's the way it should be," said Asa seriously.

Robbie said, "That was some piece you wrote about him for *The Voter*. Where'd you get all that information? Thought nobody knew anathin about him."

"Daow, that was only after us kids gut through with 'em. It wasn't too long after ah class he turned hermit."

"Talk about kids frigging with people's bones," muttered Olive.

The place was beginning to thin out, many of Decatur's customers drifting down toward Front Street in anticipation of the solemn Decoration Day parade. Asa and Olive stood up. He would be saying a little piece on the Common before the true solemnities began.

~~~~~~~~~~

Breathing hard, she had climbed almost to the summit of the hill on which Daniel died in a crevice of the rock. It was not Buck Hill, atop which they lived, but another more distant spur of the great ridge known as Blackwell Mountain. It made Chrischana sick with grief to remember sending out dogs to find the body of her son. It had been she who suggested such a search. She knew he was dead; he'd been with her in spirit even as she searched for him: It was an astonishing but nonetheless subtle memory— but she was dead to astonishment now. She was numb to everything but anger. Hatred.

If she had been more literary she would have said it was tragedy—her hubris, in leaving the abusiveness of Peter in Phoenix; bringing her implacably to the losing of Daniel in Gottheim. ...She could never have come here without Daniel's committed aid. Chrischana received it as an irony. ...I should not have allowed you out walking at night. (But he would have said, *No, Mother. That was one of the best parts.*) She casts her thoughts in her own terms: *We ah in the hands of the monster God.*

...The exact place she had so loved and been drawn to by that love—Daniel gone! He was better far than Peter, better than Balder, better much than Gottheim; better than anybody—certainly far and away better than herself.... And yet it was for *herself* she grieved, *her* loss. No one else had lost anything. Especially not *Monster God*! Monster God has Daniel, everything.

You!

She was reaching for breath. *You ah a big gazillion pound ape. A gorilla.* "Any waya in the theater You waunt You sit." She hissed it.

Turning back to look out toward the village of her homecoming (but it was hidden behind a flank of Jasper Mountain), she was struck through with a great sword of beauty. There the distant slopes; framed by the tender generous spring green of all the trees about her. There. She saw a great rainbow, mostly of amethyst, glistening in pure morning air where cloud-mottled slopes of the giant stood. There early morning sunlight cast its heart-breaking shafts.

She screamed. "What good is it!?" Chrischana, who but seldom raised her voice, who had stood much, and moved from defeat to victory. Bereft.

They were all down there, somewhere, in all that great beauty, solemnly marching, some of them, marching to the Memorial Day ceremony she would shun.

It had been more than ten years since the end of the Southeast Asian war, almost 40 since WW II. She did not think of Korea or the First World War. Eloise was following along in the puddled gutter, watching and walking with the parade participants, most in uniforms of one sort or another. Starting from the parking lot of the American Legion hall they strode along Front Street toward the Common. Silent solemnity walked with them over the pavement, the feet only of these participants sounding. There were gently fluttering flags and banners, and Girl Scouts, Boy Scouts, Cub Scouts and Brownies marching in dignified little clusters. There were soldiers old and new, a few from every branch of the service, marching. These were followed by straggling townsfolk of every age and description, some wheeling strollers; gathering more as the parade passed. Eloise watched as quick wiry Libby hurried along ahead of her, then behind her, clicking off pictures with *The Voter's* camera, sometimes with careful attention to framing. Jim Nutting was ahead on the Common, Eloise knew, probably still with his green visor, but possibly not. At least his pencil would be poised. It was something he might have sent the Twitchell boy out to do, but Daniel Twitchell was ... well, Daniel Twitchell was no more.

And then she was thinking of the bunch of bones she had found, and the hidden graveyard, and the black vault, and the night it had all happened. And Eloise was thinking that she'd been saved, and that later there would be a motorcade for the legionnaires and whoever wanted to join; that volunteers would be hiking up to set right the headstones and view the new graves, decorate them with flowers. And with flags: There was at least one veteran in that bony bunch, and more remains, long buried there, from the Civil War. And then Eloise visualized the dust of the Dead rising in bodily form and clothed so bright with new flesh, themselves setting right the headstones, so that there would be nothing to do when the volunteers got there but decorate. Here was love. She thought she was through being the hard-to-get player.

And now the silence was broken again by the drummers, keeping solemn time on the march. They were passing the solid block of Gottheim's churches, white and silent and firm. And now the deep green gem of the Common opened out, its trees a-bud and blossoming, the clean streets of its margins flanked with Gottheim's proper old houses. And Eloise Patadoe tromped along.

~~~~~~~~~~~~~~~

Balder Simon had not marched down with the uniformed soldiers from the Legion Hall. He stood on the edge of the Common near the respectful gathering beneath budding branches. He was lithe, his muscular arms folded across his pectorals, wearing the uniform he wore now, flannel shirt and jeans, work boots. His hair was white blond, trimmed as though with a bowl over it, and he had a short but full black beard. Slightly behind, and touching him, stood gold and shining Gloria. She was pregnant with their child, conceived the night Daniel died. She would be telling him soon. She had to do something to console his grief. But was it the right thing? —right for her? One good thing—he had been talking to other Nam vets…lately.

The breeze ran lightly across them; it ran softly through the solemn gathering listening to the sturdy speaker in his WW II uniform. It used to be that Gloria was highly attentive to speakers, but now she scarcely heard the former Army Pfc.

" 'Not long ago I heard a young man ask why people still keep up Decoration Day, and it set me thinking of the answer.' "

The speaker was reading a modified version of Oliver Wendell Holmes Jr.'s "In Our Youth Our Hearts Were Touched With Fire," delivered one hundred years ago at John Sedgwick Post #4, Grand Army of the Republic.

Watching the aged former infantryman as he spoke, Balder could not help seeing and feeling the slippery disintegrating flesh and bones in his hands as he lifted Marine Pfc. Socotomah who had been baptized in the napalm of friendly fire. Tears streamed down his face, the tears he never cried. Not until Daniel. Daniel came and went. And now, heedless, Balder cries.

Gloria felt sure she had never seen a rural Mainer cry before. This was certainly not usual. Certainly not for Balder. She could not even be sure he knew he was crying. Possibly if he did he would stop—? She did not know. She was starting to wonder what she did know. ... *Have to stop thinking now. This is creepy.*

But it was good that Balder had been working on his little farmstead. *Daniel's farm he calls it.* But sometimes he seemed distant to her now... and more golden-bright. Like the god, she imagined. Once he said there would be another war.

In front of her Balder shifted his stance. He heard the Pfc. quoting,

> *"The day embodies in the most impressive form our belief that to act with enthusiasm and faith is the condition of acting greatly. To fight a war, you must believe something and want something with all your might. You must do so to carry anything else to an end worth reaching. More than that, you must be willing to commit yourself to a course, perhaps a long and hard one, without being able to foresee exactly where you will come out.... The rest belongs to fate."*

This Gloria heard. She was thinking about the child and all her ambivalence. And that she just did not know. ...Fate? Does anyone know what this means today? They used to know...in ...the Middle Ages. But perhaps it was an erroneous construction of the times. *Well they thought they knew a hundred years ago, too.* "Our times'll nevah be erroneous," and "How many master's degrees you got?" In memory she heard Balder say these ironical things, grinning.

Balder wiped his eyes on the shoulder of his shirt, still heedless, but he heard the old Pfc. say, " *'As surely as this day comes round we are in the presence of our dead.'* "

That's so every day, Balder thought. And sometimes they are dead ... and sometimes alive again. Painfully alive.

Chrischana. To Chrischana Daniel is dead. Everyone in her church thinks her faith has failed. Because she can't look at anybody without glaring, without that smoldering hatred. She says things like, "It's not you, it's Him. It's that monster, God." They look askance at her. But Balder knows. She has more faith than before. More than them all. She is going on with God, wrestling. Balder still believed, after all he had seen and done. It was his descriptive error, he was sure, brought that fire down. Or maybe it was a joint error. He wished it was. They said it was, the investigators but .... If there was a monster it was this life, he felt sure. God's attitude was this: As long as it's here He might as well make use of it, suffering. Suffering. When it's not around anymore He won't.

"On this day when we decorate their graves—the dead come back and live with us. I see them now, more than I can number, as once I saw them on this earth. They are the same bright figures, or their counterparts that come also before your own eyes."

Oliver Wendell Holmes had spoken again, and the people of Gottheim listened attentively. Soon the graceful blossom-scented Common would smell of acrid smoke, it's tranquility shattered by gunfire.

All the heroic deeds of the heroes of Viet Nam. They weren't the scenes that kept returning through time.... Besides, didn't Einstein say the velocity of time is not constant? For the pilots splitting the sky the war is a little bit longer but, yes, he envies them their cool distance from carnage. ...And there were more, by far, heroes ... everyone doing their job. Even the berserkers. ...But he could not count himself among—.

He looked at the soldiers standing attendance at the front of the encircling gathering, focusing on those he knew who'd seen action. *They are the only ones who know.*

"This is where we'll live," says the Marine lieutenant, taking in the linkage of sagging littered bunkers and beyond to the valley of rice paddies and endless jungle, the piled up ridges. "We'll clean it up. Make our own fields of fire. They left us a mess, but we'll fix that."

Those commemorating stood at attention, some enduring some relishing the thrill, the repetitive *bang* of the twenty-one gun salute. The white heads in the group did not flinch, but a baby began to cry. As the seven in their dress uniforms stood straight and fired down the length of the Common toward the opening where Hutchins Pond was glimpsed through a neighboring yard. There distant islands appeared and disappeared in the early fog; the reality of each island with its reflection touching one another and breaking, touching and breaking apart. The hills surrounding this greening valley with their piled up endless ridges echoed the anomalous blasts.

A year ago Gloria had witnessed the same ceremony and heeded its rendering of life in ritual, receiving it with a mind eager to embrace the life and heart of little Gottheim. Now she felt merely bewildered. She gripped Balder's arm and let loose of it to hurry away toward Beck's Bed-and-Breakfast—going to be sick. She had to find a place to vomit.

Balder turned to watch her go, puzzled. She had liked the salute last year; it had stirred her. He watched the smoke of gunfire drift off in the direction of those fields of fire and thought how his youth was truly touched with it, just as Oliver Wendell Holmes had said. And he was never the same after. His name was still Balder Simon. But it should have been something else.

The God's Cycle is set in the early mid-1980s

Guide to Characters

Asa Bartlett. Amateur historian, Congo Church clock-winder, millworker, married to Olive Lovejoy Bartlett.
Olive Lovejoy Bartlett. Caregiver, family woman, dowser, operates bed-and-breakfast, married to Asa Bartlett.
Lyman Bearce. Lumber baron, selectman, married to Rhetta Bearce.
Rhetta Bearce. Committee woman, married to Lyman Bearce.
Babette Buck. Dowel millworker, Ferddy Sessions' girlfriend.

Jeffy Decatur. Diner business owner-cook, bird hunter.

Gloria Fay. Graduate student, IICE facilitator, sister to James Fay, Balder Simon's love.
James Fay. Ski resort real estate salesman, brother of Gloria Fay, engaged to Theodora Prescott.

Harry Golding. Ski resort owner, maternal uncle of Amanda.
Julius Golding. Ski resort owner, maternal uncle of Amanda.
Amanda. Niece to the Goldings.

Jasper Mary. Historical and legendary healer, storyteller.

Israel Kimball. Town recluse, former academy headmaster, scholar.

Jim Nutting. The weekly *Village Voter* editor.

Eloise Potadoe. Artist, goatherd, homesteader.
Theodora Prescott. Mill owner, IICE participant, engaged to James Fay.
Peter Prince. Mechanic, common-law spouse of Chrischana Twitchell, father of Nathan, Benaiah, Daniel.

Robbie Robichaud. Logging contractor, father to Alvin and Ansell.
Alvin and Ansell Robichaud. Loggers, twins.

Celon Segar (pronounced Cigar by the locals). Tire dump owner.

Cindabilla Sessions. Niece to Ferddy Sessions, girlfriend of Daniel Twitchell.

Ferddy (Ferdinand) Sessions. Town worker, Cindabilla's maternal uncle, boyfriend of Babette Buck.

Hannah Sessions. Farmer, domestic worker, mother of Ferdinand Sessions, grandmother of Cindabilla, sister-in-law of Nellie Sessions.

Melvinia Sessions. Diner server, domestic worker, distantly related to other Sessions.

Nellie Sessions. Dowelmill-worker, artifact collector, aunt to Cindabilla.

Balder Simon. Vietnam veteran, millwright, son of Elda, father of Daniel Twitchell, lover of Gloria Fay and Chrischana Twitchell.

Elda Simon. Animal rehabilitator, mother of Balder Simon.

Benaiah Twitchell. Adolescent son of Chrischana Twitchell and Peter Prince.

Chrischana Twitchell. Dishwasher, homesteader, common-law spouse of Peter Prince, mother of Daniel, Benaiah, Nathan.

Daniel Twitchell. Teenage son of Chrischana Twitchell and Balder Simon, friend of Cindabilla Sessions.

Nathan Twitchell. Youngest son of Chrischana Twitchell and Peter Prince.

Like this? Try also other stories of THE GOD'S CYCLE.

Plus *Gott'im's Monster*